TAMED BY A TIGER

ETERNAL MATES BOOK 13

FELICITY HEATON

THE ETERNAL MATES SERIES

Book 1: Kissed by a Dark Prince

Book 2: Claimed by a Demon King

Book 3: Tempted by a Rogue Prince

Book 4: Hunted by a Jaguar

Book 5: Craved by an Alpha

Book 6: Bitten by a Hellcat

Book 7: Taken by a Dragon

Book 8: Marked by an Assassin

Book 9: Possessed by a Dark Warrior

Book 10: Awakened by a Demoness

Book 11: Haunted by the King of Death

Book 12: Turned by a Tiger

Book 13: Tamed by a Tiger

Book 14: Treasured by a Tiger

Book 15: Unchained by a Forbidden Love

Book 16: Avenged by an Angel

Book 17: Seduced by a Demon King

Book 18: Scorched by Darkness

Book 19: Inflamed by an Incubus (2022)

CHAPTER 1

Rain hammered down outside the window of the taxi, catching the colourful lights of the city and shimmering, and making the cars parked along the road glisten. It was strange.

August couldn't remember the last time he had seen rain.

Snow, yes.

Endless snow.

But not rain.

How long had it been since he had left the pride village high in the mountains and ventured down into the mortal world?

Years?

He leaned his right arm on the plastic that framed the bottom of the window, sighed and stared out into the night. At the rain. At the people. So many people.

The hour was late, but London was alive and buzzing.

Back home, high up in the mountains, it would be silent by now, the peace rarely broken by the sound of a roar from down in the valley as one of the big cats found prey or crossed paths with a rival.

Gods, he had always found it too quiet.

He had taken to filling the silence of the night with the song of females in his bed, their cries chasing away that dreadful quiet and bringing life and light into the darkness.

How long had it been since he had done that?

Too long.

After Cavanaugh had left the pride in his hands five months ago, he had been doing his best to run it and be a good alpha to everyone.

It was far harder than it had looked.

He closed his eyes, shutting out the busy and entrancing mortal world, and that magical rain, and huffed.

He had trade negotiations with a neighbouring pride in a little over a week and he didn't have a fucking clue what that entailed, and asking Dalton, his second in command hadn't helped. When he had grown the balls to ask him, Dalton had looked as lost as he felt. They were both learning this shit as they went along, making half of it up and hoping what they did was right, and what the pride expected.

Keeping his people happy, he could do, and had been doing well.

But dealing with land rights and trade of goods between prides?

He could wing the basics, but he couldn't risk doing that with something as important as those two things. If he screwed up the impending negotiations, the pride would probably want him out, and he couldn't allow that. He was the only heir to the position of alpha, which meant there would either be a fight between the strongest males in the pride to see who would take his place, or the pride would call upon a former alpha.

Cavanaugh.

His cousin had been raised to be an alpha, while August had been raised to play a supporting role.

Had he made a mistake by accepting Cavanaugh's offer?

Had he been out of his mind to think he could be an alpha?

He wanted his cousin to be happy though, and the damned idiot would have stuck with tradition if he had taken back the mantle of alpha, making it impossible for him to be with his mate, and beloved, Eloise, because she was born of the lower ranks in the pride.

So August had stepped in like some fucking hero.

Who was the idiot now?

He flicked his eyes open and watched the world whizz past, listening to the background noise of the driver's radio, the methodical clunk of the windscreen wipers and the whoosh of the tyres as they cut through the water on the road.

Still, Cavanaugh was with Eloise at last, and for better or worse, August was in charge of the pride.

It should have been grand.

Alphas were never short of female company, which was exactly the way he liked things.

Only life had a way of kicking him in the balls.

Sure, he had three prides trying to palm off females onto him, and several of the high-ranking females in his own pride making valiant attempts to bed him.

But now he didn't have time for that shit.

Or the inclination.

Gods, he missed the old days. He would have bedded them all, maybe more than one at a time, using them to chase back that chilling silence of the night when his thoughts travelled paths he didn't like, leaving him feeling cold inside, strangely empty.

He would have had his fill of them, used them to keep his bed warm all hours of the day and night, just like many of the pride's alphas before him.

Hell, he had thought it would be a perk of the position, had imagined himself rolling in more females than ever, at least double the number he had used to invite into his bed.

Now, he had no lack of females who wanted him, but no desire to do anything with them.

His life had truly gone to Hell.

The stress of running the pride had him awake most nights, poring over documents and tearing his hair out as he tried to figure out what to do about the thousand issues and projects piled up on his desk, and busy every hour of the day, taking visits from members of the pride and hearing their problems.

His every moment, every breath, was dedicated to getting the pride back on their feet. It had been five months to the day since he had helped Cavanaugh defeat Stellan to free the pride of his vicious tyranny and had taken over leadership in Cavanaugh's stead.

Five fucking months.

He hadn't had the energy to even think about sex in that time, let alone actually do it.

And to top it all off, someone had started the rumour that he was sleeping with Dalton.

Like hell he was.

Dalton was a good male, and one hell of a looker, and always had his back, but neither of them swung that way.

The only reason August hadn't crushed that rumour was because Dalton was seeing a female from the lowest ranks, and if their families found out, they would probably castrate him and castigate her.

No way he was going to let his best friend take the hit like that just because he was bucking tradition. August was behind him one hundred percent, would do whatever it took to help them be together, just as he had for Cavanaugh. He never had been cool with some snow leopard traditions.

Now he was caught up in them himself. As alpha, he could bed all the lowborn females he wanted, but he was expected to pick from the highborn or somehow find his fated one among the elite, the snow leopard female who had been made for him, if he ever chose to settle down.

If.

August had no intention of doing such a thing.

He sighed. Dalton would probably leap at the chance to settle down with the female he was seeing. It was obvious his friend loved her. The male pined for her when they were apart, and couldn't keep his eyes off her when the pride were celebrating something and everyone was gathered in the square of the village.

August should have turned him down when he had offered himself as his second in command. Maybe then Dalton could have found a way to be with his female. Now, because of his elevated position, he was expected to choose a female from within his own social sphere.

He couldn't do this without Dalton though.

His friend was indispensable, kept him sane when he was losing his mind, and pulled him up whenever he tripped and fell. He was more than a right hand man. He was vital.

So vital that August had left the pride in his capable hands while he flew halfway across the world to London.

August hated to admit it, but it felt fucking good to be away from the pride and his responsibilities there.

He hadn't come all the way here for pleasure though. He had come on business.

The business of saving his arse.

He looked up at the redbrick warehouse to his right as the taxi pulled up outside it, at the bright neon sign that hung above thick steel doors.

Underworld.

August slipped the driver his money, grabbed his duffle bag and opened the door. He stepped out onto the wet tarmac, slammed the door and stared up at the sign as the car pulled away, leaving him alone in the night, rain pouring down on his face.

Damn, it felt good.

Cleansing.

He closed his eyes and let it wash over him, let it carry away some of his nerves.

The doors of the club opened and laughter burst around him, and he watched the two females staggering away, heading towards the main road.

He eased inside the nightclub in one fluid motion before the door closed, not touching it, and stilled in the darkness. The twenty-foot-wide corridor opened out a short distance ahead of him into a huge space. Flashing colourful lights stuttered across the black wooden bar that ran along the right black wall of the club, and the dance floor that filled the rest of the space to the left. It was still busy, close to one hundred people writhing against each other to a heavy rock beat. Halfway up the height of the building, a balcony ran around three sides of the dance floor, only absent above the bar. A few couples were making out up in the booths he could see, and more than one of the enclosed spaces had the curtain drawn across to give the occupants some privacy.

Cool air washed over him, and his nerves vanished, his head growing a little light as he breathed it in. What was in the air conditioning vents? Whatever it was, it was good.

He drifted towards the bar, suddenly feeling mellow and as if he didn't have a care in the world. The pride? Not a problem. Trade negotiations? Whatever.

A low growl sounded ahead of him.

It rankled a little, and he instinctively flashed fangs, although he wasn't sure where the threat was coming from.

There were a lot of different species in the club, and he smelled more than one shifter.

And also the shifter he had come to see.

"Sherry, check on the boss," Cavanaugh's deep voice rang through the room, cutting through the thumping music.

A pretty blonde of indiscernible breeding bounced along the bar towards him, bringing his gaze with her, and he frowned when she stopped and his eyes settled on the one who had threatened him.

A big, very pissed off looking, male with tousled short sandy hair and enough muscle packed beneath his white shirt to make it clear August wouldn't win in a fight against him.

At least not in his human form anyway.

The male's golden eyes glowed, his face in shadow as lights twirled above him, shifting colour.

"Kyter?" The one called Sherry touched his shoulder and he snarled at her. She snatched her hand back, looked over her shoulder, and hollered, "You deal with it. I dealt with him last time!"

Cavanaugh set a tall glass down in front of a male at the bar, heaved a sigh and turned towards him.

Froze.

His grey eyes widened, locked on August, a ripple of surprise crossing his face a second before he scrubbed a hand over his softly-spiked silver hair and stomped towards him.

"I have this," he said, voice a gruff growl as he approached the female. She squeezed past him and went back to serving the customers. He reached the male at the end of the bar and slapped a hand down on his shoulder, and didn't release him when he growled at him, baring short fangs. "This is my cousin, August."

The blond male looked him up and down, curled a lip and pivoted on his heel, striding away from Cavanaugh.

Cavanaugh rolled his broad shoulders, stretching his white shirt even tighter across them, and offered an apologetic smile. "Kyter isn't good with male shifters wandering in unannounced."

It was a territory thing.

Now that he knew the male's name, he knew why he had reacted so badly to his presence.

Kyter owned Underworld, had taken Cavanaugh in a few years back when he had left the pride after Stellan had defeated him. August eyed the blond. According to Cavanaugh, he was a jaguar. Highly territorial.

It explained the pheromones the club was pumping out in the air conditioning.

Cavanaugh grabbed a tall glass, stuck it under one of the pumps, and pulled him a pint. He set it down on the bar and nodded towards it.

"Sit, and tell me what the hell you're doing here." His cousin leaned on the bar near the drink.

August walked to it, slid onto the stool and set his duffle down beside him. "I should have called first."

Cavanaugh's lips curled at the corners, and his grey eyes twinkled. "You could have just called."

It hit him hard that he could have. He could have used one of the pride's satellite phones and called Cavanaugh to talk about how the hell to handle trade negotiations.

Instead, he had got on a plane and flown all the way to London.

"It's fine," Cavanaugh said, his smile gaining a sympathetic edge. "Even alphas need a break from time to time. Look at my father. He was always away on 'business'."

The feeling that had been building in his gut, a vicious sort of squirming that had set him on edge, eased on hearing that and seeing in Cavanaugh's eyes that his cousin thought he had done nothing wrong by leaving the pride.

He hadn't realised that it had been a need to get away, a need to have some space, that had put him on the plane and had him flying away from the pride, from his responsibilities, though. It hadn't even crossed his mind until Cavanaugh had said it.

He had been so focused on a need to speak with Cavanaugh that he had been convinced the only way to do it was face to face.

August looked down at his beer. Fucking idiot.

Cavanaugh slapped his shoulder, and August was thankful he had chosen his left, and not his right. Damn thing was still healing after their fight against Stellan.

"Don't beat yourself up. A break will do you good."

He nodded, lifted his beer to his lips and took a swig. Damn, it was good. Not as good as the homebrew they had at the village, but it was still good. Different. It was freezing cold for a start, not warmed over a fire.

"I lasted all of a month before I took a break." Cavanaugh grinned at him, and August couldn't tease him about that.

Cavanaugh had been pushed into a position that had taken him away from Eloise, had separated them because of their status, and it had almost killed him.

It was good to see the old Cavanaugh back though, the one who smiled and laughed. It made everything August had done worth it, and everything he was going through.

"Sometimes I feel as if I'm drowning in all the requests, and appointments… and all the bigger picture shit too… like this trade negotiation in eight days." August swigged his beer again, savouring the crisp coldness of it that turned to heat as it slid down into his stomach.

Cavanaugh rested both forearms on the black bar top and his eyes searched August's, his face a mask of seriousness.

"When were you thinking of going back?"

August shrugged. "The day after tomorrow. That's the next flight."

His cousin pulled his phone from the pocket of his black trousers, swiped over the screen as it illuminated his face, making his eyes more silver than grey, and then shoved it away again.

"Make it the one after. It's only four days… but it will be good for you."

He found himself nodding, because four days sounded heavenly. He needed some space, some time to get his head straight and learn from Cavanaugh about how to run the pride. He would still be back in time for the meeting.

Cavanaugh was right.

Some time away would be good for him.

He hadn't noticed that the club was emptying until a door off to his left, beyond the end of the bar, opened, throwing a flash of white light across the room. He glanced there, and couldn't stop the smile that curved his lips when he saw the pretty brunette stood with her back to the door, her golden-brown eyes searching the length of the bar.

Eloise.

She spotted him and her smile lit up her face. She lifted her arm, pulling up the hem of her plain dark t-shirt with it, and waved.

Cavanaugh's dark grey gaze swung her way and brightened, a corona of pure silver ringing his pupils as he saw his mate.

Eloise hurried towards them on August's side of the bar, and rocked him by pulling him into a hug the moment she was within reach. "I thought I smelled company."

Cavanaugh growled at his mate, or was it him? It didn't stop August from hugging her back, squeezing her tight and earning another low snarl from his cousin.

Eloise released him, leaned over the bar beside him, caught hold of the front of Cavanaugh's white shirt and pulled him towards her. She kissed him. It was one way of shutting his cousin up. Cavanaugh grabbed her under her arms and hauled her over the bar.

August snatched his beer a split-second before Eloise's legs swept through that spot, saving it and holding it at shoulder height. Damn good job he did too, because Cavanaugh twisted her into his arms, so her feet arced across the bar right in front of August. He was on the verge of lodging a complaint when Cavanaugh kissed her.

Damn, it was good to see them.

It made him feel that everything was worth it, *really* worth it, and that he had made the right decision, because they were so happy together.

But it also triggered that strange cold feeling that had kept him awake at night for decades, that had bothered him since the day he had realised Eloise was Cavanaugh's mate.

He would never have what they shared.

It was rare for his kind to find their fated ones, because they were always another snow leopard, and their numbers were low and their prides spread far and wide. Most snow leopards settled for falling for another of their kind and mating with them, but the bond they shared was nothing compared to the bond between fated mates.

A bond Cavanaugh and Eloise shared.

One that made him a little envious.
One he felt sure he would never find for himself.

CHAPTER 2

Maya walked beside her brother, taking in everything as the sun cast beautiful evening colours across the sky above the city. A city. She had never imagined she would see one with her own eyes, especially one as large as London.

Grey grumbled something, but she ignored him. He was probably complaining about walking for the millionth time.

She had convinced him to ditch the taxi, mostly through begging and a small dose of guilt trip when she had mentioned how badly she wanted to experience a city before they continued their journey.

She felt bad about that.

It wasn't like her to resort to such tactics with her brother, or with anyone.

She glanced up at Grey. He towered above her, a wall of muscle and darkness, glaring at anyone who dared to look at her, his ice blue eyes as cold as Antarctica. The evening breeze ruffled his unruly silver hair, brushing fingers through it. Beneath the ice, and the anger, she could see the beginnings of worry.

He was worried about her.

She had asked him to keep things upbeat during their journey, and he had managed it so far, had held his tongue and not mentioned how he was against what she was doing. He had even only made one attempt to convince her to go against their oldest brother's, Byron's, and their dead parents' wishes and break the contract between her and the Altay alpha.

She hated it whenever he tried to make her do that.

He sounded so much like Talon, his twin. Talon had been telling her for years to call things off, had relentlessly tried to convince her, to the point where it had started to hurt and she had almost wavered.

Her parents had promised her to the Altay male though, a contract that had been formed at her birth, and she needed to honour their memory and that promise.

It was hard sometimes though.

She didn't want to leave the pride.

Not because she feared becoming a mate to a male she had never met.

Because she feared for Grey.

She gazed up at her brother, soaked in the way his eyes leaped around the city, looking at everything, and that ripple of excitement she could feel in him, one that echoed her own feelings.

She wasn't the only one who had spent the majority of their life in the pride village.

Grey had been stuck there too, because of her.

Their parents had given him the role of protecting her, one that always went to the son who was next in line from a daughter. Grey had relished the role when she had been a cub, doting on her, growing closer to her while he drifted away from the pride. Their mother had once told her that she had been the best thing to happen to Grey, and Maya hadn't understood until she had finally noticed the way some of the pride treated him.

The role was both a blessing and a curse for him.

When their parents' had died, and Byron had taken over the role of alpha, Maya had only been young, barely a century old. Byron had decreed that she wasn't allowed to leave the pride village, and had taken Grey's freedom together with hers.

She was glad that with her leaving, he might finally have some freedom, could experience the world Talon got to see, but she was worried too.

What was going to happen to Grey?

She brushed the back of her hand across his, and he glanced down at them, and then up into her eyes. He frowned, his pale blue eyes warming but then cooling again as he looked at her, searching hers for the reason she was upset.

She feared something terrible might happen to Grey in her absence.

Some members of the pride looked at him in a way she didn't like, a way she knew Grey had noticed, silently scorning him because of his markings, making him feel like an outcast.

Making him feel he didn't belong.

She knew he hated his colouring, that he believed his white and black markings were ugly, and not beautiful.

All because of how people at the pride treated him, and how they talked behind his back.

He was beautiful though.

She had never seen a tiger as beautiful as Grey.

His frown hardened, and he stopped, turned to face her, and lifted his hand. She didn't stop him as he swept his finger below her eyes.

"You don't have to do this," he murmured, a wealth of love in his blue eyes, mingled with hope.

"I do," she whispered, ignoring that ache in her heart that had started five days ago when Byron had announced that he was changing the plans and she was going to head to the Altay pride in the coming week.

Grey looked as if he wanted to tell her that she didn't, but he lowered his hand instead, and adjusted the straps of the pack slung over his left shoulder, cutting into his thick black coat.

His eyes shifted to his left. "You know he's going to say the same thing, right?"

She nodded, and she was prepared for that, but she still had to see him.

She couldn't go to Siberia without saying goodbye to Talon.

Grey sighed and started walking again, his long legs easily carrying him away from her so swiftly that he was at the corner of the street before she had even moved. She hurried after him, her deep gold dress flapping around her knees. She had chosen her favourite one, a knee-length affair in the empire line style, cinched beneath her breasts and capped with short sleeves.

When Grey had seen her in it, he had asked why she had chosen to wear her shield. She hadn't understood at first, but as the journey to London had dragged on, she had begun to realise what he had meant. This dress was her shield. It made her feel confident and a little brave, and as if nothing bad could happen to her.

He turned the corner when she reached him, and she looked there, her feet sticking to the ground when she smelled the jaguar who had come to the pride with Talon when Archangel had attacked them and spotted the neon sign of the club.

A big male stood outside it, his tone gruff as he spoke with the people heading inside. She wasn't sure what species he was, but he wasn't human. Black jeans and a t-shirt hugged his broad frame, and a black skullcap covered his hair. Maya figured he was the bouncer, because he matched the image she had of them from the television shows and movies she had seen.

He gave Grey a puzzled look as her brother approached him. Understandable. Talon worked at the nightclub he protected, had been there for a few weeks now with his mate Sherry, staying at her home while she became accustomed to being a tiger shifter.

Grey and Talon were almost identical, separated only by their hair and eye colour.

Maya wished that they had come out perfect twins, because then Grey would have been happy, would have been accepted.

She hurried to meet Grey at the door of the club, and smiled at the bouncer as he let them in.

That smile dropped off her face when loud music assaulted her. She flinched away, grimacing at the horrific volume of it as it rang in her ears. Grey looked over his shoulder at her, seemingly unaffected by it. There had been a few instances when he had been allowed to go out into the mortal world so it was possible he had visited such a place before and had been prepared for the onslaught.

He could have warned her.

He grabbed her wrist and pulled her into the gloom, tugging her through the busy wide corridor at the entrance of the club.

She wrinkled her nose and covered her right ear with her free hand as the music grew louder, the heavy beat shaking the black walls of the warehouse. Gods. How could any shifter work here?

Her eyes darted around, but everyone she looked at didn't seem to care about the volume, were all talking to each other. Among other things.

She passed a couple that were openly making out, the female pressed against the wall and the male's hands on her sides, skimming up and down her bare flesh. Double gods. What sort of place did her brother work at now?

Was this a club or a sort of naughty den?

The number of couples lost in each other dropped significantly as Grey reached the main room of Underworld, where bright colourful lights danced over the long bar and illuminated the bottles that lined a mirrored wall behind it. The area around the bar was packed, four rows deep of people trying to order a drink. She took in the dance floor, her eyes widening at the sight of it.

She had attended celebrations at the pride, but they hadn't come close to this.

Almost three hundred people swayed, grinded, pumped and jostled on the dance floor, a mass that moved as one, all of them plastered together, pressed up against each other. The music changed, and a cheer went up, fists pumping the air, and the dancing grew more frenetic, matching the rhythm of the guitar.

Gods.

She grunted as someone knocked her and came close to flashing fangs at them.

Someone else banging into her stopped her.

Because it struck her that she was knocking them aside.

She looked up at her brother, who mercilessly pulled her through the crowd, and then tugged on her arm, bringing her up to him, and pushed her in front of him. Her stomach met the brass railing around the bar and Grey caged her in, his body shielding her from the crowd.

Talon's jaguar friend hurried past, four bottles of something held in his hands, heading towards the right side of the bar. Sherry turned away from the brightly lit bottles of liquor that stood on glass shelves against the mirrored wall, and stilled. A smile instantly burst onto her dark pink lips and lit up her blue eyes.

Was it really only four weeks since Maya had last seen the blonde?

She looked even more beautiful now, radiant, glowing with happiness.

Maya had feared the transition from human into a tiger shifter would have taken its toll on her, but Sherry looked brighter than ever, healthier too. She warmed inside at that, glad Sherry was handling it well, and sure it was Talon's doing. Talon was probably doting on her like crazy since they had mated and bound themselves together.

"Cavanaugh, take over a moment," Sherry called over her shoulder, towards the other end of the bar to Maya's left.

Her eyes leaped there.

Landed on a huge male with short silver hair who stood with his back to Sherry, the lights playing across his broad shoulders changing his white shirt from blue to red as they shifted.

He twisted at the waist to look at Sherry.

Maya didn't hear what he said.

She didn't hear the music.

Didn't hear anything but the thumping of her heart.

She stared at the male Cavanaugh had been talking to at the end of the bar.

A male with flame red tousled hair and piercing silver eyes that captured hers as he lifted them from his beer to her, looking past the bartender.

Heat rushed through her, fire that burst to life inside her so fiercely she couldn't catch her breath, and she stared at him, transfixed, lost in those silver eyes as they turned liquid, glowed around his irises and pulled her deeper still, narrowing the world down to only him.

Who was he?

In the wake of the fire that blazed through her blood, her instincts flashed to life, sweeping through her in a devastating wave that stripped all control from her.

She snapped and snarled at the females near her, baring her short fangs at them as a need seized her and drove her to obey it.

A need to fight.

She growled at Sherry through gritted teeth, her fangs slicing into her gums as they elongated.

Sherry backed off, her blue eyes shooting wide as she distanced herself.

No.

On a low growl, Maya leaped onto the black bar, and swiped at her, claws cutting through the air. Sherry ducked beneath her blow, narrowly evading it. Maya's hackles rose, the urge flowing stronger, driving her harder. She needed to fight. She needed to make sure every female in the vicinity left.

This was her territory now.

She would make that clear.

She opened her mouth to roar.

Someone's hand slammed down over it, and she struggled as strong arms hauled her backwards, dragging her off the bar. The male held her harder, wrestled with her and managed to restrain her arms, pinning them to her sides. She bit into his palm and he growled at her, a warning she wanted to heed but couldn't manage to obey.

She needed to fight.

"Calm her the fuck down or you are both out of here, family or fucking not," a male voice barked and she snarled at the owner of it—the jaguar. "Get this shit under control."

"Come with me," Sherry said and Maya struggled harder, needed to reach the female and fight her.

Needed to make this her territory.

Grey grunted and his grip on her tightened, and she flinched as pain arced like lightning through her bones. A show of strength. He was stronger than her, but she wouldn't let him stop her. He could break her bones if he wanted. She would fight.

She kicked at him, battering his shins.

He bowed backwards, bringing her legs up and making it impossible for her to reach him.

Maya lashed out at everyone in her way instead.

All it did was help her brother by scattering everyone in his way, giving him an open route to take as he followed Sherry.

As she drew closer to the male with the fiery red hair, the need to fight grew stronger, drove her out of her mind and terrified her, leaving her feeling trapped inside her own body. She clawed at Grey's arms, cutting through his coat and scoring his flesh, but all he did was hiss through his teeth. His grip on her remained too strong for her to break.

She needed to break it.

She needed to fight.

The scarlet-haired male's silver eyes tracked her until she was level with him, and then casually he looked back down at his beer and resumed speaking with Cavanaugh.

Cold swept through her in response.

All of the fight flowed out of her and she slumped in Grey's arms, reeling but unsure why.

Why?

As Grey carried her into a bright white backroom and the door shut behind them, awareness of what she had done slowly crept in, closing in around her.

Grey set her down, and she stared at the ruined sleeve of his black jacket as he tended to the wound beneath, inspecting it. She had done that. She had lost control.

Her amber eyes widened and leaped to Sherry.

Gods. She had tried to hurt Sherry.

"I'm sorry," she muttered, horrified by what she had done.

"It's fine… but… I'm not sure what just happened." Sherry offered her a smile, a small one that spoke of confusion as clearly as her eyes did. "Is it because I'm a tiger too now?"

Maya wouldn't answer that question.

Grey focused a little too hard on his wound, avoiding it too.

Boots striking metal off to her left had her head whipping that way, the instinct to fight rising again but for a different reason this time. Grey was injured. She needed to protect him.

Talon stopped on the bottom step and stared at her. "What are you doing here?"

The tension that had started to leave her on seeing it was only her brother approaching amped up again, making her muscles tight as she came to face him. His amber eyes were hard, demanding. He raked his fingers over his short black hair and huffed as he stepped down onto the floor, and strode towards her.

She looked over his clothing. Was he working as a bouncer now? He wore the same black t-shirt and jeans, and boots combination as the male she had seen guarding the door. She didn't like the thought of Talon protecting the entrance of Underworld. It was dangerous.

"I needed to see you before I continued my journey."

His face darkened. "Journey?"

Damn. Byron hadn't told him. That bastard.

Grey growled from beside her. "He's sending her to the Altay pride now."

"What the fuck?" Talon barked and took a hard step towards her, all the fires of Hell raging in his golden eyes. "Son of a fucking bitch."

He turned to her, seized her upper arms in both of his hands and hunkered down, so he was eye level with her.

"You don't have to do this."

Gods, he sounded like Grey.

"Tried that," Grey mumbled and Talon frowned at him. "She isn't listening."

She isn't listening to reason. That was what Grey had wanted to say.

She was listening, but reason didn't factor into this. Her parents had promised her to the Altay pride male and she had to go through with it, because if she didn't, her pride would be shamed by her actions and would lose standing in tiger society.

"I need to get back to work." Sherry managed a single step towards the door that led to the nightclub before Talon had her swept up in his arms, his lips on hers.

Maya looked away.

Ignored that pang of jealousy that made her chest feel too tight.

The moment Sherry was gone, Talon heaved a long sigh. "I'm going to kill Byron."

"No," Maya snapped, her gaze whipping up to meet his amber eyes. She shook her head, wanted to say something else, something to defend Byron's decision, but she couldn't.

Because it had shaken her.

She loved him, but sometimes she shared Talon and Grey's view of him, their belief that he saw her as a sort of bargaining chip, a way of establishing a stronger connection with another powerful pride.

A present he could give to their alpha.

She tried not to feel that way, had fought it for years, but now she couldn't feel any other way.

She could only feel that he didn't truly care about what was best for her, not as Talon and Grey did.

He only cared about what was best for the pride.

She told herself that it was how things should be, that he was alpha now and had a responsibility, one that extended beyond his family.

His decision to send her to the Altay pride now, when she wasn't due to go there for another two decades, when she reached her two hundred and fiftieth year, had come as a shock though.

A blow.

Archangel's attack on the pride had left them wounded, and weakened. Vulnerable.

Byron had told her that he was doing it to keep her safe.

As much as she wanted to believe that, there was part of her that believed he had an ulterior motive. They had lost many people in the battle, and he wanted to strengthen their position in tiger society quickly, so no one would challenge him as alpha. He had already sent out two females to other prides, and had taken two brides in exchange.

She was to be the third.

Her move to the Altay pride would ensure their support for Byron, making it difficult for anyone within her pride or outside it to challenge him without facing fierce opposition.

It was a power play.

One that would also ensure the safety of her pride.

If she could do that for them, then she would go through with it, whether she wanted it or not.

"Does Byron know you're here?" Talon cut into her thoughts, tugging her back to reality, and she shook her head. He looked to Grey. "Did she pull those kitten eyes on you?"

Grey rolled his right shoulder. "Maybe I just figured it might be a good thing... that we could talk some sense into her."

That wasn't going to happen.

She had always wanted to be of use to the pride, had tried to find the place where she fitted in and could be of help. Now she knew what she needed to do, how she could help her pride, and she was going through with it.

"It's worth a try." Talon smiled faintly. It grew into a full blown one when he came over to her and pulled her into a hug, and ruffled her hair. "I'm glad you came. Saves me from having to go to Siberia to drag your arse home."

She stopped trying to swat his hands away and looked up at him. He would do that for her? The look in his amber eyes confirmed that he would, and that it was going to take a lot to convince him to let her go now that she was here.

She didn't want to fight Talon, or Grey, but she wasn't going to let them stop her.

She wouldn't break with tradition.

She didn't want to be traded like a commodity, forced to be someone's bride, but she wanted the pride to be strong and Byron to be safe.

"Can I not just enjoy this time with you?" she whispered, and the smile that had been rising onto his lips faded, the light in his eyes dimming as he dropped them from Grey to her.

She hated that look.

She always had.

It hurt her whenever she looked into any of her brothers' eyes and saw pain in them.

It killed her that she had caused it this time.

She pushed away thoughts about Siberia, and her own pride, and focused on her brothers, and the building around her.

She had been so excited when she had been walking through the city with Grey and when they had entered the nightclub, seeing a world that so closely matched the one she had seen on the tablet that Talon had snuck into her home so she could watch television and movies without Byron knowing.

Now she could see it with her own eyes.

She wanted to enjoy this time with them, in this world of mortals.

Even though it was a little overwhelming.

The scarlet-haired male from the bar shimmered into her mind and heat travelled through her limbs and bloomed in her chest.

He was a little overwhelming.

Just thinking about him had the instinct that had seized her in the bar rising back to the fore to wrest control from her, a deep desire to attack any female in the vicinity and drive them all out.

Maya didn't want to think about what that meant.

In two days, she would be in Siberia.

She would be bound to the alpha she had been promised to at birth.

And nothing could change that.

Not even him.

CHAPTER 3

August was finding it impossible to concentrate on anything Cavanaugh was saying about prides and appropriate greetings that should happen at the start of a meeting with one.

He had been doing just fine, scribbling notes like a damn school kid in the pad opened on the round white plastic table in front of him, until forty-three minutes ago, when he had been talking to Cavanaugh about his failing sex life and waxing lyrical about all the females he had bedded in those halcyon days before he had become alpha.

He had caught the most bewitching scent he had ever smelled, an intoxicating blend of cinnamon and snow, spicy but soothing, and had turned his head in time to see the black-haired female from last night standing in the entrance of the kitchen.

Her striking amber eyes had been as round as twin suns as she had stared at him.

The big male who had been with her last night, a wall of muscle and menace with silver hair and icy eyes, had been swift to usher her away, and August had heard him mutter about finding somewhere else.

Ever since then, he had been wondering where this somewhere else was that he had taken her.

"Earth calling August."

He blinked himself back to Cavanaugh, who sighed as he stood, the legs of his chair scraping on the tiles as he pushed it back.

"You need some coffee?" His cousin crossed the small distance between the table and the basic kitchen to August's right, plucked the jug from the machine and frowned as he lifted it. It was almost empty. His dark grey eyes shifted back to August. "I can make a fresh pot."

August didn't think coffee was going to save him.

He had tried concentrating. Really tried. He looked down at the pad and grimaced at the doodles all over it. His fingers had obviously wandered as much as his mind. He hadn't taken in anything Cavanaugh had told him.

"I think I need some air." What he really needed to do was clear his head and evict the dark beauty from it, but that probably wasn't going to happen.

Something about her had him fired up.

Which was a monumental fucking achievement given the recent death of his libido.

He pushed his chair back, stood, and scrubbed a hand across his tired eyes.

"Give me fifteen?" He looked to Cavanaugh, hoping his cousin would be alright with the break, because he wasn't going to be much use to him if he couldn't find his focus again.

Cavanaugh shrugged. "Go for it. I'll check on Eloise."

August wanted to pick him up on his choice of words. Check on Eloise? It was pretty crap code for fooling around with his mate. He couldn't hold it against Cavanaugh though. His cousin should have been in bed, enjoying sleeping with his mate, but here he was teaching August the ABCs of running a pride. If Cavanaugh wanted to use the break to make out with Eloise, that was fine with him.

He nodded and walked out of the room, his feet heavy as he tried to figure out where to go and tried not to think about where Cavanaugh was going.

Five months without sex.

Hadn't even thought about it.

Not a single urge.

He turned right and followed the corridor, intending to head up the smaller staircase to the roof.

The scent of cinnamon and snow teased his senses.

August followed it through the building, unable to stop himself from tracking her. It led him to the stairs and then downwards, towards the ground floor of the nightclub. Heat bloomed in his blood and his pulse quickened, his senses sharpening as he focused on her scent, homed in on it and ignored everything else.

Hunted her.

Five months, and now he couldn't think of anything else.

Gods, he wanted her.

He had wanted her the moment he had set eyes on her.

It was just the sudden release from the pressure of being an alpha. That was all. Cavanaugh was right and being away from the pride was doing him good. He felt free again, energised, and back to his old self.

A player again at last.

That was the only reason he wanted the beautiful female who smelled of cinnamon and snow, who set his blood on fire and had his heart beating faster whenever he saw her, and a deep urge to seize her blazing through him.

Hell, if he headed into the club tonight, he would probably want any number of the females who lined the bar, could scratch this itch with his choice of them and be done with it.

Maybe he would scratch the itch a few times.

Make the most out of being away from the pride.

His libido was bound to take a hit again the moment he returned.

He might as well enjoy it.

His feet carried him downwards.

Towards her.

Did she belong to the male he had seen her with? The two were close, and the silver-haired male guarded her as if she was precious to him. It would be just his luck if she was. The first female he had wanted in months, and she belonged to someone else.

A door opened and closed off to his left as the large white room came into view and he glanced there.

The male.

He slowed his pace as the male approached, and nodded as he jogged up the stairs towards him.

The male suddenly stopped. "Have you seen Talon? We were looking for him but we can't find him or Sherry."

August had met Talon once, shortly after he had arrived. "The only time I've seen Talon, he was on the roof, sunbathing with the pretty bartender."

The male snarled at him. "That bartender is my brother's mate."

Brother. Interesting.

He looked the male up and down, seeing the family resemblance. The male shared Talon's features, smelled similar in a way, but the scent of the female lingered on him. He wanted to growl at that.

He held himself together, clamped down on that need, and said, "Did you bring your mate to meet your brother?"

The male's silvery eyebrows rose high on his forehead and then dropped, a crinkle forming between them and a flicker of confusion crossing his pale blue eyes. "Mate?"

"The black-haired female I saw you with." August tried to say that as casually as he could while the need to rip the male apart warred with a sudden bout of nerves that the male might see right through him and rip him apart instead.

His eyes turned a shade darker blue but shone a little brighter around his pupils. "My sister. We're just stopping by to see Talon on our way through London."

Through London?

"Where are you going?" August regretted that question the second it left his lips.

The tiger's face darkened, his eyes narrowing as he frowned at August, and his voice became a low growl. "That's none of your business."

August stood his ground, unwilling to let the tiger intimidate him. The male stepped up to him, his eyes on August's the whole time, and then huffed and moved on, heading up the stairs.

Moody son of a bitch.

It didn't stop August from wanting to know where they were going.

He wasn't sure why he needed to know.

Maybe it was just that itch to fuck she had ignited in him.

He wanted to know her schedule so he knew whether he had time to win her over and bed her.

He looked down to his left.

At a door in the white wall.

A door that would lead to her.

He kept his eyes locked on it as he took the last few steps, as he turned, and as he walked towards it, drawn to it, and to her.

He needed to see her again.

Needed her.

He reached out and gripped the steel handle, and paused, breathed through a sudden rush of feelings, a collision of fear and desire that was foreign and unsettling. Five months without sex wasn't long enough to dampen his charm, and definitely wasn't long enough to make him forget all the right moves to make, the ones that would ensure she fell into his arms and into his bed for one wild night with no strings attached.

So why the hell was he on the verge of having a panic attack?

It was just sex. That was all he wanted from her. All he wanted from anyone.

He shoved the door open.

Froze.

Gods.

She was beautiful.

The tiger standing opposite him in the makeshift gym lifted her head and stared at him through bright amber eyes, her pupils dilating as she spotted him.

That feeling ignited again, fiercer than before, sending a hot shiver over his skin.

She dropped the barrel she had been attacking in the middle of the large space and growled at him.

Fired every damn instinct he had and triggered a need to dominate her, to drive her into submission.

August bared his emerging fangs and growled right back at her.

He wasn't sure whether she would understand the message—that he wasn't going to submit to her.

She was going to submit to him.

She went deathly still, not a single muscle twitching, her eyes locked on him.

His heart accelerated, his breath coming quicker as he waited.

Waited.

Maybe this was going to be easier than he had thought and she was just going to roll over for him.

Two hundred pounds of tiger suddenly leaped at him.

Maybe not.

CHAPTER 4

Maya turned the moment she sensed someone enter the room, ready to snap and snarl and drive them away, because this was her room.

Her territory.

Her toys.

She wasn't going to share them with anyone, had already driven Grey away when he had been the one to suggest she shift and work off some energy.

She stilled when she spotted the scarlet-haired male standing in the doorway.

Heat flared, rushing through her, and she dropped the barrel and growled through her fangs at him.

Hers.

He was hers.

His silvery eyes brightened, pupils dilating to swallow that precious colour as he stared at her in silence, not moving a muscle.

His heartbeat drummed steadily in her ears, not a trace of a tremble in his powerful athletic body.

He was fearless as he faced her.

As he growled.

Maya was too fired up to heed that order he issued, too far gone to withdraw.

This was her territory.

Hers.

And so was he.

She sprang at him and he didn't have a chance to move. Before he could even twitch, she had landed on his chest, her front paws on his shoulders, and he was going down. He grunted as they landed, her weight slamming into his gut, and she felt an echo of his pain.

Mine.

She growled in his face, flashing her fangs.

He would submit to her.

In a lightning fast move, he had flipped her onto her back and was off her, back on his feet and a metre away. She rolled onto her paws, a growl rumbling through her chest, the need to force him into submission pounding through her together with anger that he had dared to disobey her.

She slowly circled him and he kept pace with her, maintaining the distance between them, those pure silver eyes not leaving hers, tracking her every move so she couldn't get the jump on him again.

"You're playing a dangerous game," he husked, voice like honey, a smooth purr that had her shivering with delight.

She knew that.

But he didn't know just how dangerous this game was.

For both of them.

Part of her was dimly aware that she needed to stop, that she needed to shift and leave, before the hungers he ignited in her became too strong for her to fight and she surrendered to them.

Fight.

She wanted to fight.

She hunkered down on her front paws and growled again, a need to battle the male growing within her, spreading tendrils through her until it had total control over her and all she could do was watch.

He smiled slowly. "If you want to do things this way, I'm game."

He reached over his head, grabbed the back of his dark red t-shirt and pulled it over his head.

Maya swayed a little as the glorious sight of him hit her, stunned her and left her reeling, her mouth watering and that hunger flaring hotter, filling her with a need to run her tongue over all that flesh.

Scars littered his chest, faded and silvery, but it was the one on his right shoulder that arrested her eyes. It was thick, cutting across his muscle, and dark pink. Still healing. He had been in a battle recently. She shivered inside at that, her need growing as she imagined him fighting, as she realised he was a warrior.

A strong male.

Tamed by a Tiger

"You look as if you need a good workout." There was a flash of something wicked in his silver eyes as he said that, something that told her he wasn't talking about fighting.

He was talking about the other thing.

Her heart quickened, blood thundering at just the thought.

He fingered the button of his black jeans and her eyes fell there, that heat growing fiercer as he slowly popped each one, teasing her. It burst into wildfire in her veins when he reached the last one and casually, shamelessly, shoved his jeans down his legs.

Gods.

She growled at the sight of him, unable to contain her reaction.

That smile widened, grew a little cocky.

She had seen countless males naked at the pride before and after they had shifted, more than just her brothers, but none of them had been like him.

He was glorious.

He would be hers.

She leaped at him.

Before she could reach him, he had shifted, stealing her breath away.

Beautiful lush pale silver fur with black broken rings covered his sleek form, his tail thick and bushy, and almost the length of his body, and his eyes gained a gold shimmer.

A snow leopard.

The sight of him caught her off guard.

Left her wide open.

He collided hard with her and tackled her, knocking the air from her as they landed with him on top. She growled and twisted, slapped him hard with her front left paw and then her right, battering his face. He snarled back at her and made a lunge for her throat, and she swiftly bucked up, pushing her paws against his neck and his shoulder. The right one.

He hissed and distanced himself, but only for a heartbeat.

He sprang at her again, and she was ready this time, rose onto her back feet and reached with both paws, managed to get them around his neck as his landed around her ribs. He snarled as she brought her head down, whisker close to sinking her fangs into his throat, and twisted downwards, breaking her hold.

Maya growled and followed it with a hiss as she swiped at him, her ears flattening against her head.

He leaped backwards, only a few feet, and eyed her, studying her closely.

She bared fangs at him.

27

He would submit to her.

Those golden-silver eyes shimmered with heat and amusement, an answer to her question. He would not.

She was damned if she was going to submit to him. He was male, but she was stronger, her heritage giving her an advantage over him.

The male leaped at her again, springing high into the air, and Maya hunkered down and kicked hard, propelling herself towards him with all the speed and strength she could muster. He grunted as they collided, but kept his wits, his fangs snapping close to her face as he tried to claim her neck.

Never.

She twisted in the air, using her weight against him, pushing him down into a vulnerable position, and growled as she landed on him. He hissed, flashing fangs, and kicked at her, catching her flank with his claws. She snarled and snapped her fangs at him, because if he wanted to play rough, she could do that, and he would regret it.

She brought her paw down hard, smashing it into his right shoulder.

He growled through clenched fangs, ploughed his back paws into her stomach and kicked hard, shoving her off him to land awkwardly on the floor. She was on her paws a second later, rising up onto her back ones to meet him as he rose onto his and tried to grab her.

She tried to stand taller, instinct driving her, awareness that he would win if she didn't maintain the upper hand when they grappled. Her balance faltered, and she stumbled back a step and her front dropped. The male's left paw landed on her shoulder and drove her down, and he landed on top of her back.

No.

On a feral growl, she kicked up, driving into him, forcing him off her. She ignored his warning growl, the one that demanded she submitted to him, and brought her right paw around and her claws out.

He hissed as they cut across his shoulder.

Red marred his beautiful silver and black fur.

She thought he would back down now that one of them had drawn blood.

It only made him fight harder.

He snarled and launched at her, and she rolled, letting him hit her front rather than her back. He pinned her down, his gold-silver gaze bright as he stared into her eyes, and then he snapped his fangs at her and pushed his weight down on her. She brought her back legs up, tried to kick him but he was at an angle to her, his lower half too far away from her for her to hit.

His head came down.

Maya hooked her right paw around his head and rolled left, pulling more of his weight on top of her.

In range of her back legs.

He broke her hold and leaped off her, and she kept rolling, hit all four paws and came into a crouch, breathing hard as she kept an eye on him. He circled her, breathing hard too, the cut on his shoulder dripping crimson down his leg.

The part of her that was still aware of the world, that one existed beyond this room, beyond him, whispered that this was dangerous, that she couldn't do this, that she was promised to another.

She didn't want to be promised to another.

She wanted the male who had been made for her.

She leaped at him, and he rose onto his back paws to meet her, welcomed her into his paws and grappled with her. She managed to get her fangs into his neck and satisfaction poured through her, the instinct to fight him and force him into submission fading as she held him in her teeth, not breaking the skin.

Her guard dropped again.

The world whirled past her and suddenly he was behind her, had her pinned to the floor in a hold.

His teeth against the scruff of her neck.

Maya stilled, went lax in his grip, fear rushing through her to douse the fire, leaving her cold.

But he was gentle as he held her in his fangs, didn't make a move to bite her or hurt her.

The door in front of her opened.

Talon walked in. "Grey said you wanted to speak with me about something."

He lifted his head and stopped dead.

Stared at her.

And then his face darkened, a tempest raging in his glowing gold eyes.

And he roared.

CHAPTER 5

For the second time in less than an hour, August had a tiger leaping at him.

Only this time, it was four hundred pounds of very angry male tiger.

He quickly released the female, fear he would hurt her by accident bolting through him, and had just pushed away from her when the male hit him.

Hard.

He wasn't strong enough to fight the male, weighed barely the same as the female in his snow leopard form, and was far smaller than both tigers.

He was going to have to rely on speed rather than strength in this fight.

But he wasn't going to back down.

He tried to gain some space, but the male was on him before he could move an inch, his teeth clamping down hard on the back of his neck. The male growled and shook his head, rattling August's brain around in his skull and sending fiery pain shooting down his spine and over his shoulders.

Fuck.

He tried to hold his snow leopard form but the pain drove him to shift back. He grunted as he part shifted, managed to claw it back at the last second and revert back to his snow leopard form.

Just as the tiger tossed his head to the left and sent him flying through the air.

August grunted and hissed as he hit the wall of the gym and landed on a treadmill, the centre console hitting him in the stomach.

Talon snarled and came at him, huge paws raking through the air where August had been, and was now gone. The tiger hit the console instead, a frustrated growl rumbling from between his fangs as he stood on his back paws looking at it.

August kept low, sneaking around the side of the machine, his long tail twitching as he stalked the male. Stupid tiger.

Talon huffed, blowing his cheeks out, and August grinned inside.

Until Talon's golden eyes snapped down to him and he realised the tiger had been aware of him the entire time, had been feigning confusion to draw him out into the open.

Son of a bitch.

A huge paw slammed right into his face, driving him nose first into the rubber belt of the machine. Pain splintered over his skull as Talon pushed his weight down on it. Fuck.

Someone growled.

The female.

He looked towards her, his instincts flaring again, a desire to fight and win, to show her that he was strong and able, could handle a tiger twice his weight and size.

Talon growled at him, as if he had heard his thoughts, a warning that it wasn't going to happen.

That victory would go to him.

Not a fucking chance.

August pushed his paws into the floor and tried to wriggle backwards, out from under Talon's paw. Claws pressed into his head, dug into his skin, snaring him. He hissed and stilled.

The female growled again.

Stalked towards them.

Either it was his imagination or there was a flicker of blue around her pupils.

It was gone when he blinked.

So was Talon's paw.

The male turned towards her and chuffed, making a low coughing sound in his throat. She bared her fangs at him.

August eased back, trying to distance himself from the male while he was occupied.

Talon pounced on him.

"Enough!" Kyter's voice cracked through the room like a whip.

Talon landed on August's head.

Before the male could attack him, he was gone and Kyter stood before him instead, his gold eyes on fire with the fury August could scent on him.

Loose grey sweats rode low on his hips, his sandy hair sleep mussed.

Talon's roar must have woken him.

The big tiger growled and Kyter swung to face him, bared short fangs and stared him down.

"You want to find a new fucking place to work?" Kyter said, his tone measured, calm but filled with a threat, one that Talon obviously felt the male would carry out because he backed off and shifted.

August followed him, gritting his teeth as his body transformed, bones adjusting beneath his skin as his fur disappeared. He knelt on the black rubber floor, hands planted against it, and blew out his breath and sucked down another, fighting to steady his pulse as it raced.

When he tried to straighten, every muscle ached in protest, fire burning through his legs and across his shoulder. Damn.

He clutched it and grimaced as his hand slipped on the blood.

The little kitty had definitely left a mark on him.

He looked at her, and frowned.

She hadn't shifted back.

Kyter's eyes came to land on him.

August grabbed the console of the treadmill, pulled himself onto his feet and lifted his gaze towards Kyter. Fuck. Cavanaugh stood in the doorway beyond the jaguar, Talon's brother beside him.

The look in his cousin's grey eyes warned that Kyter wasn't going to be the only one dealing out a little telling off where he was concerned.

"You want to explain what the fuck is happening here?" Kyter snapped, his words a thick growl.

"That's my fucking line," Talon barked and Kyter shot him a glare. August dished one out to the bastard too. Talon glared right back at him. "What the fuck was just happening?"

"We were blowing off steam." It sounded reasonable and it was partly true.

He glanced at her.

She still sat near the corner, her head bent. Ice washed through him. Had he hurt her after all? He had tried to be gentle.

Talon growled at him. His brother echoed it.

"Look. I found her in the room fighting barrels and I figured maybe she wanted to fight someone for real. I can take it." He risked another glance at her. "She's such a little thing, she wasn't exactly going to hurt me."

That seemed like a stupid move for his mouth to make when both brothers glared daggers at him.

"Maya," Talon growled.

She shrank back, and August wanted to rip the arsehole a new one for frightening her.

"Leave her alone." August stepped closer to her, catching the shifter's attention again. "I started the fight, so blame me if you want. Leave her out of it."

"That isn't going to happen. Grey." Talon looked from him to his silver-haired brother. The male nodded and moved, heading towards Maya. Talon's amber gaze dropped to her. "Have you changed your mind?"

Grey flanked her, approaching her slowly, stripping off his t-shirt as he neared her.

She didn't lash out at him, didn't look at him either.

She kept her head bent, even when she shifted back and Grey helped her put his t-shirt on to cover her nudity.

August didn't even get a damn glimpse of her curves.

Maya drew down a slow breath, pushed her long tangled black hair from her face, and carefully rose onto her feet, coming to face Talon.

She tipped her chin up, her gaze steady and unwavering. "I have not."

Changed her mind about what?

Talon's amber gaze darkened, the black slashes of his eyebrows dropping low. "You don't have to do it."

Her soft voice was calm and even, strong and determined, as she said, "I do. My plans haven't changed. This male was right and I just needed a fight. I feel fine now."

That stung a little.

That was all he was to her?

Someone to fight?

A convenient male in the right place and the right time for her to work off some aggression?

Like hell he was.

He turned towards her.

Cavanaugh collared him, his grip firm on the back of August's neck, and marched him towards the exit.

"I need a moment with my family alone," Talon said, his expression so cold he made August's homeland look positively tropical in comparison.

Kyter held the door open for him and Cavanaugh.

Just as it was about to close behind him, August glanced back into the room.

At her.

She lifted her chin and ice ran through his veins and down his spine as she spoke.

"I leave for the Altay pride as planned tomorrow night and nothing you do can change my mind, Brother."

CHAPTER 6

"What really happened?" Talon rounded on her the moment the door had closed.

Maya's eyes leaped to it, and then down to the pile of clothes on the floor. Clothes the snow leopard had left behind. His scent surrounded her, teased her senses in the most delicious way, together with the memory of the feel of his fangs against the nape of her neck. She shook that memory away, not strong enough to withstand its tempting whispers right now.

Her brother took a step towards her, but she refused to look at him, couldn't while she was trying to figure out the answer to that question herself, denying the one that kept coming to her. There had to be a different reason, something not so crazy.

Not so painful.

"Sherry said you became aggressive and tried to attack her in the bar when you first arrived." Talon's words ran over her like an icy torrent, sucking the heat from her blood and leaving her cold. She had foolishly hoped Sherry wouldn't mention it to her brother, that she would have put it down to them both being a tigress because she was new to their world and didn't know any better. Her brother moved another step closer, narrowing the gap between them. "It isn't like you, Maya... so I need to know what's happening between you and that snow leopard."

Gods. She wasn't really sure of that herself.

She had caught the emotions that had flashed across his handsome face when she had told Talon that she had merely needed to fight, and that she was fine now. She hadn't meant to hurt him with her words. Or had she? Had she wanted to drive him away?

To protect him.

Or to protect herself?

"Tell him," Grey whispered at her side, and she lifted her eyes to meet his.

The gentle look of affection in them warmed her, chasing some of the chill away, and eased her heart. He was right. She needed to tell Talon what had happened, if only so she could relieve some of the weight on her chest and breathe again. She was closest to Grey, but she was close to Talon too, had sought comfort from him before, and he was knowledgeable in the way of both tigers and hellcats, far more so than Grey. When Talon had first learned of their mixed blood, he had researched hellcats, had learned all he could about them.

Maybe he would have answers for her.

The thought of learning what her behaviour meant terrified her though. Why was this happening to her now, when she had never felt such fierce and consuming urges before?

She had never felt the need to fight the females at the pride for territory.

But she couldn't shake that need here.

She swallowed hard, linked her hands in front of her chest, and fought for the words, to push past the fear that Talon might react badly and put it all out there and trust that he would help her, would be as gentle with her as Grey had been when she had bravely told him.

"I need... I'm so confused, Talon. I don't want to hurt people." She silently cursed the way her voice warbled, always hated it when she sounded weak, even in front of her brothers.

She blamed the way everyone treated her for that hang up, coddling her as if she was some princess and fragile, and not the tigress she was inside. Her brothers always viewed her that way, couldn't see the female she really was, or how they drove her mad with a need to escape.

Sometimes, that need became so intense she could only obey it.

How many times had she snuck out when everyone was sleeping, heading high into the mountains that surrounded the old pride village?

Her brothers would have killed her if they had discovered what she had been up to and had caught her.

Gods, it had felt good though. It had felt glorious to run wild in her tiger form, to do reckless things like leaping broad crevices in the rocks with the threat of a long fall into the valley or hunting the huge stags that shepherded their groups of does around the forest.

She had even run into Kincaid's wolf pack once, had snapped and snarled at them as they had growled at her.

It had been exhilarating.

She had felt alive.

But when she returned, she felt something else.

Trapped.

With each adventure, the hatred she had for her confinement grew.

Sometimes, she wished she hadn't been born into her family.

Gods, it was wrong of her. She loved her brothers, all of them, with all her heart, yet she couldn't stop herself from resenting Talon because of his freedom and Byron because he held the key to her cage and kept her locked in it.

All she wanted was to taste that freedom and to break that cage.

"Maya," Talon whispered, earnest and tender, and she looked at him and dashed away the tears on her cheeks.

More came as she caught the soft look in his eyes, the pity and the love.

She didn't want to cry.

She sniffed, scrubbed the new tears away, and crossed the room to him. She checked the wounds on his chest, focusing on them, and on helping him, giving her fingers a task to complete while her mind whirled, thoughts spinning through it so quickly she wasn't sure whether she was coming or going.

She loved her brothers.

She did.

"I don't know what's happening to me," she whispered to his chest, and traced the lines of the ink that covered his left pectoral, losing herself in the design like she had so many times before. She had asked Talon if she could have a tattoo once. He had laughed, and then bluntly told her no.

Maybe she would sneak away from Underworld and get one.

"I know," Talon murmured, his hands coming down on her shoulders. "You're afraid… you don't want to do this."

She glanced up at him, and then back down at his chest. "I do."

"You don't need to lie to us." Grey moved closer, and some of her strength faded, the tempting thought of just letting her brothers be strong for her stealing it away.

"I'm not afraid of what I'm going to do," she murmured and poked at a wound, one long slash that darted across Talon's chest. He didn't even flinch. The cut was deep, but it was healing. She lifted her eyes to meet his amber ones. "I'm afraid of what I might do."

He rubbed his thumbs across her shoulders and sighed. "So tell me what you're feeling… and I'll do my best to help."

She nodded.

Sucked down a deep breath.

"I feel so out of control. I need to fight... and it frightens me. When it seizes me... I can't stop myself, Talon."

He pulled one hand away from her, scrubbed it over his mouth and then pushed his fingers through his short black hair. "Do you just need to fight, or is there a reason you want to fight?"

She averted her eyes, pulled her courage up from her toes, and pushed the word out. "Territory."

He tipped his head back and muttered, "Fuck."

Indeed.

"Grey brought me to the room because I needed to do something." She twisted the front of her t-shirt into her fists, battling that need. It was weaker now, background noise, but it was still there. It wouldn't be long before the urge seized her again. "I thought I might feel better if I took out that aggression somehow."

Talon huffed. "That isn't going to happen. You're not going to stop feeling this way until—"

"Don't say it!" she snapped, her entire body tensing as she squeezed her eyes shut, as if she could block out reality and make it go away by doing such a thing.

Both of her brothers sighed.

Talon's hand cupped her cheek, and he slowly raised her head, but she refused to open her eyes and look at him.

"Maya..."

She shook her head. "This doesn't change anything. *He* doesn't change anything. I heard him talking to the other snow leopard... about females. He wouldn't be interested in me... and I'm promised to another."

"You're promised to a bastard," Grey bit out.

She flicked her eyes open and scowled at him, but she couldn't deny it. The reports on the male she was promised to were dire, frightening in a way. Although they had all come through Talon and Grey, so she felt certain they had embellished whatever rumours they had heard in an attempt to put her off going through with it.

"He's not the gentle boy our parents knew." Talon caught her shoulder again, holding it firmly this time.

"But he is the male our parents promised me to. I'm bound by a pride pact to him, and I have to do it... to honour them." She shirked his grip. "I've known about it my entire life and I'm willing to go through with it."

Or she had been.

Until she had met the snow leopard.

August.

Life was too cruel, bringing her mate into her path now, when she was on her way to Siberia.

Talon's face grew darker, the black slashes of his eyebrows drawing low over his bright amber eyes, forming a crinkle above his nose. She didn't like that look. Never had. Whatever he was about to say, he hated it.

Despised it.

"It's starting to sound a lot like you're doing some messed up version of tiger tradition…" he sneered, his voice a low snarl that sent a cold tremor through her. "Sacrificing yourself for the sake of someone stronger… but you're not fucking weak, Maya. You're strong and you don't need to do this! Byron can go fuck himself."

Her instinct was to shrink back a step in the face of his fury, but she held her ground, rooted her feet firmly to the floor and refused to give in to that desire. Because it would make her look weak, and her brother was right.

She was strong.

"I'm not following tradition." She kept her tone even and measured, calm in the midst of the storm crossing Talon's face now, a tempest born of his feelings about the traditions of their kind, and the grief and guilt that still haunted him after what Jayna had done, sacrificing herself so he could live. She wanted to comfort him, but he would see it as an act of submission, would believe she was listening to him at last and would do as he wanted. "You are right, Brother. I am strong… and it is taking all of that strength to do this for the sake of the pride and our alpha… our brother."

That tempest grew fiercer, flaring in his amber eyes and turning them gold.

She dropped her gaze to his bare chest again, because she couldn't bear to look into them and see that anger, that pain, and know she was the cause of it. It would wreck her, tear down that strength she was clinging to in order to do this, and push her closer to giving in and doing as her heart really wanted— running as far as she could from Pyotr, the alpha of the Altay pride, and into the arms of a snow leopard.

"I've heard things about him." Talon's tone was so dark that it chilled her, and she couldn't stop herself from looking at him, and watching that darkness cross his face, destroying all the light that normally shone in his eyes when he looked at her. He looked like a different male. A stranger to her. She had never seen him so angry. She shook her head, silently begging him not to tell her. He denied her. "The alpha you're going to wed… he's done terrible things, Maya. *Terrible* things. Shit I don't even want to tell you because I don't want you hearing it. His pride is brutal, and he leads them to it. They wiped out one of the neighbouring tiger prides for no godsdamned reason other than to fight. He is not a good male… and I know that if our parents were alive, they would have broken this off regardless of the damage done to our pride's reputation and standing within society."

His words were little more than a snarl at the end, one that told her exactly how he felt about what she was doing and the male she was going to wed.

And exactly how he felt about Byron.

Talon blamed him for what she was doing. Grey did too.

Didn't they know they were only making this harder on her?

She didn't want to go to Siberia, but if she didn't, the pride would be put in a difficult position, and Byron would be vulnerable. He needed this alliance. The pride needed it.

It wasn't uncommon for tiger prides to fight each other over territory, and she had heard about the battle between Pyotr's pride and the other one when it had occurred three years ago. The other pride had moved too close, encroaching on the Altay pride's territory. She was sure that was the only reason Pyotr had sent his males to war. The tiger council hadn't punished the Altay pride for it, and they would have if the attack had been without reason and had therefore broken the law.

Talon was just trying to frighten her again.

"The snow leopard—"

"Don't!" She cut Talon off, couldn't bear hearing him talk about August, not when she was wavering, on the verge of falling. She needed to be strong, needed to do what was right for the pride.

It was hard though.

Made all the harder by meeting August.

She craved him, even when she knew she shouldn't. She wanted him, even when she was promised to another. Every instinct she possessed said to make him belong to her.

She couldn't.

He didn't want to belong to anyone.

She had heard it in his voice when he had been talking to Cavanaugh, when he had been speaking of all the conquests he'd had and how much he had enjoyed them. He didn't want to be tied down to a single female.

She knew a little of snow leopards.

Unlike other shifter species, they could only find their mate within their own breed.

Which meant whatever urges he felt towards her, he thought they stemmed from lust, and he was fine with that.

He viewed her as another potential conquest, a beauty he could bed and discard, another one night stand for his records.

That left her cold inside.

He would never understand, would never come to view her as anything more than just another female, because she wasn't a snow leopard. She would never be special to him, not as the female snow leopard was to Cavanaugh, or the elf was to Kyter.

Not as Sherry was to Talon.

She didn't want to be just another notch on his bedpost.

She cursed her hellcat genes.

Without them, it wouldn't be possible for her to be August's fated one, and she wouldn't be feeling this way, hurting from just thinking about him, pained by only the thought he might not want more than one night from her, but still drawn to him, still filled with a need to be with him, to take the plunge and risk her heart just so she could know what that was like.

It tore her in two, left her shaken and unsure what to do.

No.

She curled her fingers into fists at her sides.

She knew what she had to do.

She was promised to another, and if she didn't go through with it, her entire pride would be in danger again.

Her brothers would be in danger.

If her sacrifice could keep them all safe, then she would do it.

She would go to Siberia.

She would become Pyotr's bride.

CHAPTER 7

August couldn't think straight. Not surprising really given what he had heard. Maya was leaving for another pride, and he knew enough about prides to know what that meant.

She was going to become someone's mate.

He lifted his third beer to his lips and drank deep, hoping to kill the part of his brain that wanted to roar whenever he thought about another male touching her.

Gods, if only he could drown in beer.

That would be grand.

He lowered the glass and stared at the amber liquid as the coloured lights above the bar rotated, shining down on him, and the thumping rock music made the beer ripple.

Amber.

Like her fur.

He squeezed his eyes shut and growled through clenched teeth as he pushed his hands through his red hair, shoving it back.

Damn it.

She was beautiful. Gods, she was more than beautiful. She was perfect—strong, curvy, a little confident and courageous when she needed to be—but whatever pull he felt towards her, it couldn't have become anything anyway.

It was better this way.

It was better it ended now before it had even started.

Cavanaugh had given him the pride, and that meant he couldn't go around doing as he pleased.

He definitely couldn't take a mate from another species.

No matter how fiercely he craved her.

He had to set the example by finding a suitable female within his own species or, even better, finding his fated one among them. Hell, it wasn't as if he wanted to settle down anyway. He wasn't looking for a mate. He really wasn't.

He was just all shades of fucked up because of the stress of running a pride. Being away from it was loosening the hold that stress had on him, made him feel his worries were hundreds of miles away, and he was free. That was the only reason he wanted Maya. It really was.

Shit.

He knocked the rest of his beer back and pushed the empty glass away from him. It left streaks of water on the black bar top and he stared at them as the coloured lights played across them, making them shimmer. When they turned orange, he saw her eyes, the way she had looked at him in that room, and how bright they had been when they had been fighting, tangling with each other.

She wanted him.

Fuck, he wanted her.

Cavanaugh stopped near him. "You okay?"

No. He was leagues from okay. He couldn't even see okay in the rear-view mirror.

He nodded. "Fine."

The look Cavanaugh gave him said he could see through the lie to the truth—that he was falling apart.

Because of a female.

This wasn't like him.

It was just the stress. It was.

It had nothing to do with how beautiful she was, how she fired him up and had him out of his mind with just a look, just a damned glance in his direction.

"Just get me another beer," August muttered.

His cousin's sensitive ears picked it up over the loud music and he took the glass and moved away, returning a few minutes later with a full beer.

August grabbed it, raised it to his lips and drank it down in one go.

It still wasn't enough to kill the part of his brain that was fixated on Maya and that she was leaving.

Leaving.

He slammed his fists down on the bar top, ripping startled shrieks from the nearest females and earning a black look from his cousin.

Fuck.

August shoved the glass away from him. It toppled and spun, before rolling towards the edge of the counter. Cavanaugh caught it before it fell, and set it back down.

"I'm cutting you off," his cousin growled.

August wanted to growl right back at him, wanted to ask him not to do it, but he didn't have the energy to do either of those things. He stared at the bar in a stupor, an image of Maya dancing through his mind, a replay of fighting her and how good it had felt.

How *right*.

Shit. The more he drank, the more that stupid part of his brain tightened its hold on him, dragging him down.

He let his head fall forwards and didn't even flinch as his forehead hit the bar.

He was starting to see why Cavanaugh had ditched the pride in exchange for his freedom, and the freedom to choose his female.

August rolled his head to one side, so he could see the females to his right as they lined the bar, vying for the attention of Cavanaugh and Kyter as they all tried to get served at the same time.

He had the freedom to choose his female.

It wasn't as if he wanted to be tied down to just one of them.

He wasn't Cavanaugh.

He studied their faces and picked out the beautiful ones. He could have any one of them. All he had to do was turn on the charm. What he felt for Maya was the same as what he felt for any female he desired. It was lust. Plain and simple. She had just been the first female to stir that in him after five months without sex.

She had just been the trigger.

The way he reacted to her didn't come as a surprise either.

She was forbidden fruit, promised to another.

That was the only reason he wanted her this badly.

She was beautiful, forbidden fruit.

And he wanted a taste.

It was the only reason he wanted her more than he wanted the females around him, but that feeling would pass if he started the ball rolling, flirting with one of them. He would get over it. He would.

He pushed himself up and straightened out his appearance, neatening his red hair and undoing one more button on his black shirt to show a little more muscle.

One of the females at the bar glanced his way and flashed a flirty smile in his direction.

It was working already.

He smiled right back at her and looked her up and down, a slow leisurely glide over her body. Her tight black dress emphasised wicked curves and breasts that would more than fill his hands, and her pouty cherry red lips promised to feel great around his cock.

So why the hell didn't he feel anything as he looked at her?

Why the hell was he thinking about Maya?

Maya in that dress, looking like a present ready for him to unwrap.

Maya's lips painted red and lush, ready to wrap around his aching shaft.

Maya's amber eyes flashing at him in that way that said he was going down, that she was going to make him submit to her.

Fuck.

He glanced at the clock on the wall to his left above the optics, and growled when he saw it was already gone midnight.

Maya was leaving today.

August shoved away from the bar and froze.

What the hell was he doing?

He sucked down a hard breath.

Growled low when he caught the scent of cinnamon and snow.

He was hunting Maya.

No fucking way he was letting her go.

He rounded the end of the bar. The female who had been flirting with him stepped into his path, her smile bright. He walked straight past her, tracking Maya's scent. She was here, in the club. Another growl curled up his throat. If a male was so much as looking at her, he was going to rip them to shreds.

He prowled through the heavy crowd, need twisting tighter inside his chest, making it hard to breathe as he searched for her.

He needed her.

He needed to see her again.

Would go mad if he didn't.

His fingers flexed and clenched at his sides as he stalked her, unaware of what his body was doing, aware of only a crushing need to find her.

A group of males pushed across his path, scattering the people ahead of him.

Revealing her.

Gods. His breath left him in a rush.

She stood at the edge of the dance floor with her profile to him, a creamy-gold dress hugging her breasts and flowing from beneath them to conceal her curves and cover her thighs, her sleek long black hair a contrast against it.

A fucking angel.

She glowed in the bright lights, seemed to shine as he stared at her, absorbing her beauty as she watched the dancers, a look of fascination on her face.

He had never been much of a dancer, but some stupid part of him wanted to get onto the dance floor and bust some moves so she would look at him like that.

As if he lit up her world.

She didn't notice as he slowly approached her, his heart beating harder with each step closer he came to her, rushing so fiercely he genuinely feared he might pass out. What was it about this bewitching female that had him ready to fall at her feet?

Ready to beg her to accept him as her male?

He shook that ridiculous need away. It was just lust. She was beautiful forbidden fruit.

"What are you doing here?" he hollered over the loud beat of the music.

She tensed and whipped around to face him, her amber eyes wide and lips parting with the shock he felt ripple through her. Those entrancing eyes leaped around the room, swiftly taking in her surroundings. Looking for someone?

It dawned on him.

Her brothers.

She wasn't meant to be in the club.

"Don't... don't tell them." She stepped towards him, which did all kinds of crazy shit to his brain, and his body. Holy fuck. He inched his left leg forwards, so she wouldn't see just how badly she had affected him with something as innocent as her moving closer to him and speaking to him. "I just needed this."

He looked around at the club, trying to act nonchalant when she had him fired up to the point of pain already and she hadn't even done anything. "What is *this*? It's just a nightclub."

She moved another step closer. He bit back a growl and curled his hands into fists at his sides, and then jammed them into the pockets of his black jeans, stopping himself from reaching out and grabbing her as he wanted to. Gods, he wanted her in his arms. He wanted to feel her pressed close to him.

"I've never been to one before."

Her words were so quiet he almost didn't catch them above the music.

August wanted to laugh at that. Only she was deadly serious.

"Don't get out much?" He smiled at her, expecting her to berate him or call him an idiot or something.

She shook her head.

His smile faded.

Was she like some of the females at his pride and had chosen to spend her entire life in her pride's village, far away from the frantic mortal world?

The look of longing in her amber eyes as they roamed back to the dancers told him that it wasn't the case and a slow burn started in his blood.

She hadn't chosen to stay away from the world—she had been locked away from it, held in the village against her will.

He couldn't hold back the growl that rumbled through his chest at the thought someone had done such a thing to her, shutting her in a cage, stealing her freedom from her.

"Your family are arseholes," he barked, his blood on fire now as he thought about her brothers, a need to find them and beat the shit out of them blazing through him.

They would pay for what they had done to her.

She glared at him.

"I'm not going to apologise." He stepped towards her, slowly closing the distance between them. "Not for what I just said."

He took another step.

"Not for being angry that some son of a bitch kept you locked away."

Another step.

"Not for what I did in the gym."

He closed the gap between them and stared down into her beguiling eyes as she gazed up into his, a trickle of fear running through her emotions. His heart beat harder, his own fear rising as he struggled to hold her gaze and narrow the world down to only her, until she was the only one in it with him.

The only one who mattered to him.

"And I'm not going to apologise for this either."

She gasped as he wrapped his arm around her waist and lifted her up, and he swallowed it in a kiss as he claimed her lips.

August banded one arm around her back and clutched her bottom with his free hand, holding her against him as he kissed her, sweeping his lips across hers and coaxing her into moving. She remained frozen against him, and that fear began to grow stronger, whispered that he had been mistaken and she really had just wanted to fight him.

And then she moved.

Her lips twitched against his, her movements restrained at first, but she grew bolder, until she was a wild little thing in his arms, her mouth fierce on his as she kissed him hard. He groaned when she thrust her tongue between his lips, angled his head and met her, driving her back into submission as he stroked his tongue along hers, teasing her with it. She moaned, tensed the moment she loosed it, and he felt her shock.

It lasted all of a second before she was lost again, kissing him deeper, fighting him for dominance that he refused to give her. Her kiss was rough, a little clumsy at times, but he didn't care, because by the gods, she tasted divine and felt so right in his arms.

He held her closer, sung sweet praises to his ancestors when she moved in his arms and her hands came down on his shoulders. She fisted his shirt, held it so tightly he feared it might rip apart, but he still didn't care, wouldn't give a fuck if she tore it right off his back right there, as long as she kept kissing him.

Her grip loosened and he moaned as she brushed her hands up his shoulders, teased his nape with her light fingers, and then pushed them through his hair. Damn. He growled, lifted the hand that held her waist to the back of her head and buried his fingers in her fall of black hair, and clutched it as he kissed her harder, deeper still.

His heart thundered against his chest, matching the beat of her own as it drummed against him.

Sweet fucking gods.

He had never felt so alive, so overloaded with feelings. It felt as if he was going to drown in them, as if they were going to keep building inside him until he couldn't contain them, until they burst and shattered him.

He wouldn't care, not if Maya kept kissing him.

Not if she was his.

Eyes landed on him.

August broke away from her lips and growled at the male, warning him not to look at his female, warning him away.

The male moved on, heading into the throng of people on the dance floor to his right.

He turned back to Maya, his gaze falling straight on her kiss-swollen lips.

He leaned in to capture them again.

Maya pushed out of his arms and staggered back a few steps, breathing hard, her amber eyes wild as she looked at him and lifted a trembling hand to those lips he wanted to claim.

"I… I can't do this."

Those lips that had just given him so much pleasure pierced him with the ultimate pain.

August growled at her.

She broke past him, her head bent, and he turned in time to see her disappear into the crowd, frantically pushing people aside as she ran from him.

Like hell he was letting her get away.

CHAPTER 8

Maya kept her head down as she fought the crowd, desperate to put some distance between her and August. Kissing him had been a mistake. She should have stopped him, shouldn't have let him do that to her, but she had foolishly thought herself strong enough to handle it.

She wasn't.

Kissing August had only made her realise what she was sacrificing for the sake of her pride, and the safety of her brothers.

It was killing her.

She sniffed back the tears, refusing to let them fall, and pushed onwards, determined to escape before she did something she would truly regret. The people in her path slowed her progress, most of them refusing to move, forcing her to find another route as she tiptoed and looked for the door that would lead into the backroom.

It wouldn't be enough to escape August.

She knew that, but she still kept pushing towards it, an ache building in her chest as she ran away from him.

Ran away from the one male she wanted to run towards.

"Damn it," she muttered and pushed a male aside.

He growled at her, but she paid him no heed, kept on pushing and shoving, desperate to escape.

Even when she knew she couldn't really escape the one thing she wanted to.

The need to honour her parents and protect the pride would continue to bind her hands, would have her returning to the path that would take her to Siberia, no matter how fiercely she fought it.

It broke her heart.

She wished she had the courage to refuse to go to the Altay pride, but the risk was too great, and she would never be able to live with herself if her freedom cost Byron his life, or put the pride in danger.

She shrieked as someone grabbed her from behind.

A hand came down over her mouth, muffling it.

August.

His masculine earthy scent filled her senses, had her purring inside and that need to fight stirring again, the need to stake a claim on him as her territory.

Mine.

No. He couldn't be hers. He could never be hers.

Not even if she turned her back on her promise and risked it all.

He had made that clear when he had been talking to his cousin.

He had said he didn't want a mate.

She tried to break free of him as he took hold of her wrist, his grip like iron, squeezing her bones and sending a dull ache up her arm. He refused to release her and dragged her through the crowd, his focus fixed firmly ahead of him. She looked there, afraid he was taking her to the backroom.

A shadowy set of stairs loomed ahead of her, close to the back wall of the club, leading upwards.

She glanced over her shoulder at the door near the bar.

He was taking her away from it.

She looked up the stairs as they reached them, at the darkness, the unknown.

Where was he taking her?

She dug at his fingers, trying to get hers beneath them so she could loosen his grip. He growled again and held her tighter as he pulled her up the stairs, into the gloom. Her pulse picked up as she stumbled on the metal steps, his heavy footsteps ringing around her, a determined clip to them as he tugged her along behind him.

Music thumped around her, quieter in the stairwell, but loud as they reached a balcony above the dance floor.

August pulled her left, along the wide balcony, past empty booths on her left, and one that had a thick curtain drawn across it.

Her pulse went wild.

No. She couldn't be alone with him. She couldn't bear it.

He reached the final booth and pulled her into it.

The moment the heavy velvet curtain was closed behind him, he twirled her so her back was against the black wall. His mouth came down on hers, his kiss like fire as it seared her, burning away her fragile restraint.

He stepped into her, pinning her to the wall, his hands claiming her hips and holding her there.

She had to stop this madness.

Maya kissed him back, couldn't stop herself as he went to war on her defences, breaking them all down and leaving her weak against him, and against herself. She wanted this, needed him with a ferocity that frightened her.

He mastered her mouth, bending her to his will, stoking that side of her he had awoken the moment she had set eyes on him. She growled and seized control of the kiss, clutching his head in her palms and holding him at her mercy. He groaned, the sound like music to her ears.

It ripped control from her grasp.

He was hers.

Hers.

She had failed to make him submit to her once. She wouldn't fail again.

She gripped his hair and kissed him harder, earning a husky moan from him that sent a shiver over her skin and made it feel hot and too tight. He palmed her backside, and she trembled and moaned, the wanton sound of it shocking her, but she was too far gone to care. His strong hands kneading her flesh sent another wave of heat through her, one so fierce she couldn't stop herself from rolling her hips against his.

A rigid length of steel met her flesh.

Gods.

Her breath left her in a rush.

All that heat, that fire, pooled low in her belly and she found herself rubbing against him, a need to feel him controlling her.

He groaned and lifted her, and she wrapped her legs around his waist and gasped as he pressed into her, pinning her back against the wall, making her feel every hard inch of him.

She trembled at the feel of it, at the urge that burst to life inside her, a powerful need to touch him, to lay her hands on his flesh and feel what she did to him.

It overwhelmed her.

Panicked her.

She stilled in his arms, her lips frozen against his.

What was she doing?

August kissed down her throat, slowly sweeping his lips over her flesh, searing her and trying to wrench control from her again.

This was madness.

Yes.

"Madness," she whispered.

August lifted his head and stared into her eyes, confusion shining in his silvery ones.

"You're handsome," she said, voice distant in her ears, her words hollow. "I want you… need this moment of madness before I go on with my life."

He frowned at her.

She faltered. It was stupid, but she needed to keep going, needed to say something to justify what she was doing and make herself believe it.

"I'm not your mate." She held his gaze, fielding another confused look. "We both know snow leopards can't find their fated one outside their species, so this is just desire… we just want each other… that's all this is."

Was she trying to convince herself, or him?

She wasn't sure what she was doing anymore. Fear was at the helm, driving her to say something, anything, that might make it possible for her to do as she wanted for once, and not end up hurt by it.

His silver eyes dropped to her mouth.

He swooped on it and kissed her harder than before, until there wasn't a part of her that didn't sing with the pleasure that rolled through her.

She could do this.

One night of madness.

One moment of doing what she wanted.

Of being with her fated one.

She looped her arms around his neck and kissed him, tried to keep up with him as it grew more heated, fiercer and faster, until all those worries that had been building inside of her went rushing out of her, forgotten in the heat of the moment.

She groaned and tipped her head back when he broke away from her mouth and kissed down her neck, his breath hot on her skin.

"Gods, I need you," he murmured against her breasts, sweeping kisses along the neckline of her dress above them.

She knew. She could feel it in him and could sense the staggering depth of that need had startled him. Confused him. It built inside her too, drove her to keep going, until they were both sated at last.

He dropped to his knees before her and looked up at her, a corona of gold around the dark abysses of his pupils. A tremor wracked her, that need cranking tighter, and she swallowed hard.

Was she really going to do this?

His eyes eased down her body, growing hooded as they fell lower.

She really was.

With shaking fingers, she clutched the skirt of her dress and inched it upwards.

Her reward was a feral growl and his hands on her thighs, driving her mad with a light caress as he skimmed them upwards, chasing the hem of her dress and then dipping beneath it. The trembling grew worse, so fierce she feared he would notice it. He moaned as he reached her backside and palmed it again, and then kept pushing upwards, lifting her dress.

She pulled it up for him, her breath coming faster, heart racing in her ears, drowning out the music.

August's gaze seared her as he raked hungry eyes over her legs, tracking the hem of her dress as she kept pulling it higher. When she revealed her cream panties, he swallowed hard.

Stared.

She started to lower her dress.

He growled and seized it, pushing it higher up her stomach. She tensed when he leaned in, but the moment his tongue swept over her stomach, following the line of the elastic of her underwear, she sagged against the wall, letting the fiery tingles wash through her.

A groan issued from his lips and he kissed lower, his hands easing down her sides. She trembled again as he hooked his fingers into the waist of her panties, her breath coming in short gasps as anticipation built inside her, colliding with the need to make it stronger, until she couldn't keep still, thought she might go out of her mind if he didn't touch her soon.

He gently slid her underwear down.

When they reached her knees, he kissed down from her belly button, igniting a fire inside her that burned so hotly it stole her breath entirely.

The first brush of his tongue between her thighs had her crying out so loudly she feared someone would hear.

She clapped her hand over her mouth and moaned into it, tingles rushing through every inch of her in dizzying waves as he stroked her with his tongue.

Gods.

"Fuck, Maya... you taste so damn sweet."

Those words almost undid her.

She glanced down at him, still holding her mouth, her eyes wide.

Fuck.

The way he was looking up at her, his eyes reflecting his desire, devouring her as he licked his lips, sent a tremor of pleasure through her.

She needed him.

Needed more from him and only him.

His eyes darkened and lowered, as if he had felt that need in her and he wanted to fulfil it.

Her panties reached her ankles.

He lifted her left foot and eased them over it.

She waited for him to set her foot back down.

He didn't.

He placed it over his shoulder, spreading her legs, and delved between her thighs, sending her shooting into the stratosphere.

Maya wasn't sure whether to keep her mouth covered to muffle her cries or grab hold of August with both hands. She shook against the wall as she fought to remain standing under the onslaught, the delicious stroke of his tongue through her flesh and the way he teased her pert nub at the end of each one.

He growled and licked harder, and she couldn't stop her thighs from trembling against him.

It was too much.

She hadn't been prepared for this.

She hadn't expected it to feel this good.

Her free hand came down hard on his head and she couldn't stop herself from gripping his hair, from holding him tightly as he licked and stroked between her thighs, sending her flying onwards, upwards, towards Heaven.

She growled as need hijacked control of her body and had her rocking against his face as he devoured her.

Oh gods.

She tipped her head back, clung to him and cried into her hand as lightning whipped through her, striking hard and fast, and leaving her shaking from head to toe. Her heart pounded in her head, blood rushing in her ears, as she fought to hold herself together, quivered fiercely. Stars winked across her closed eyes.

She really hadn't been prepared for that.

August's strong hands caught her waist as her knees buckled, holding her upright and against the wall.

He lifted his eyes, scorching her with his gaze, flooding her with a need to look at him too.

She slowly lowered her head, her breathing still ragged and too fast, her skin flushed all over, and hoped to the gods he wasn't going to look horrified.

Prayed to her ancestors he hadn't realised she was untouched.

His wide silver eyes threw a bucket of icy water over all those hopes, turning them into fears.

Fear that he would stop when she craved him more now than ever, needed him to keep going, to show her that Heaven she had glimpsed because of his masterful touch.

Fear that he wouldn't want what she was willing to give him.

All of her.

"August," she started.

She didn't get a chance to finish.

He shot to his feet and claimed her mouth in a bruising kiss, one that obliterated those fears and her voice with them, and stole her away from the world again.

Maya wrapped her arms around his neck and held on to him, kissed him hard and let herself go.

Let everything go.

Everything but August.

He was all that mattered.

"Maya," he whispered against her lips, sending heat curling through her as she closed her eyes and savoured the way he said her name.

It always came out fierce, even when he whispered it.

It always came out filled with need and a desperate edge, as if he would die if she didn't answer him, if she wasn't there with him.

"August," she murmured, let him hear in his name that she was right there with him, swept up and lost, and a little afraid.

He softened the kiss, slowing it down, easing back and leaving her feeling even more off balance, in danger of slipping and falling. She couldn't do that. This was meant to be a moment of sheer madness, about satisfying their needs, and nothing more.

So why did she feel as if she wasn't going to walk away from this unscathed?

Why did she feel as if she was about to break her own heart?

She pushed away from those thoughts and focused on kissing him, imagining him as he had been in the gym when he had stripped for her.

Sweet mercy, she needed to touch that body he had revealed to her, needed to revel in the feel of his muscles beneath her palms and all the strength at his disposal.

She seized his shoulders, swallowed his moan as she rubbed them through his black shirt and smoothed her palms over his chest. It was hard beneath her touch, and she could feel his heart hammering against his ribs, beating as frantically as her own. A tremor shook her as she reached the buttons of his shirt, a ripple of nerves making her fingers shake as she tackled the first one.

His kiss slowed again and then his lips left hers as he drew back and glanced down at her hands, watching her as she popped each button on his shirt.

Her heart beat a little faster with each one, the need to race rushing through her. She held it back and kept things slow, not wanting to spoil the moment.

Her eyes tracked her fingers until she opened the middle button, and then she couldn't take her eyes off the deep valley between his pectoral muscles. They drifted downwards as she tackled more buttons, taking in the rigid ropes of his stomach. Her breath hitched as she undid the final button and parted his shirt, revealing him to her eyes.

Glorious.

She licked her lips.

Itched with a need to run her tongue over every inch of him.

Her eyes dropped lower.

Every inch.

She pushed his shirt off his shoulders and he was quick to help her, tugging it off over his hands and tossing it onto the bench chair to her right. She failed to bite back the groan that rolled up her throat at the delicious sight of him and the way his muscles moved, screaming of strength, power that she wanted to feel under her hands.

The second her hands met his chest, he stilled, his face still averted, towards his shirt. She bit her lip and stroked her palms over his chest, quivered at the feel of his warm flesh and how smooth his skin was, stretched tight over hard muscle.

A growl rumbled through her.

Her male was strong.

But he would submit to her.

CHAPTER 9

His back slamming against the wall of the private booth knocked the wind out of August.

He leaned there, struggling to catch up. Maya didn't give him the chance. She dipped her head and her lips seared his chest, the light silken brush of her hair across his stomach sending him out of his mind. He half-groaned half-growled as she licked and nipped at him, swirled her tongue around his left nipple and kissed downwards, paying close attention to every single muscle on his stomach, as if she didn't want one to feel left out.

Holy fuck.

August caught her shoulders, wanting to slow her down and make sure she was alright with what she was doing.

She didn't have to do it if she didn't want to, didn't have to feel pressured into anything.

She answered him by grabbing his shoulders and shoving him hard against the wall, her head lifting from his stomach as she snarled at him, sending him a message loud and clear.

She was doing this, and trying to stop her had only pissed her off.

Another growl left her blush lips.

He frowned at her. Like hell he was submitting to her.

She stroked her tongue over his stomach, her eyes locked on his the entire time, and his knees shook as bliss washed over him.

All the fight that had flared to life inside him died.

Maybe he would submit to her a little.

Just a smidgen.

His cock twitched in approval, jerking against the tight confines of his black jeans.

Maya's golden eyes lowered to his chest, grew heated and hungry as she raked them over him, clearly liking what he had to offer.

Gods, he shouldn't be doing this, but he couldn't stop himself. The realisation that she was virgin territory should have had him being all noble and shit, spouting how it wasn't right and she really didn't want to give something so precious to him.

Should have.

His reaction had been quite the opposite.

Knowing that she was untouched, that he was her first, and she wanted him to be that for her, had only made him want her even more.

He wanted to ruin her to all other males.

He gazed down at her as she kissed across his stomach, cranking him higher with each one.

Gods, he needed her.

Maya lifted her eyes to his.

That corona of blue was back, faintly glowing around her pupils.

Odd.

He had never noticed any blue in her eyes when she wasn't aroused or angry.

She knocked that thought plain out of his head when she slid her eyes over him and they froze on his shoulder.

She straightened in an instant, a feral snarl rolling off her, her eyes locked on the wounds he bore.

Wounds she had given him.

Before he could say anything about them, she was on him, her tongue stroking over the red lines. Damn. The pure hit of pleasure that swept through him in response to her cleaning his wounds had another part of him weakening.

Somewhere in the region of his chest.

He stared down at her, reeling and feeling as if at any moment, he was going to fall.

And he was going to fall hard.

Hell, he couldn't move as she laved her tongue over the wounds, her actions screaming of a need to take care of him, to help him heal.

He must have stared a little too hard, because she lifted her head and growled at him again.

Only this time it wasn't a warning that he was making her angry.

It was pure, unadulterated, possession.

She planted her hands against his chest, shoved him back against the wall and kissed him.

Hard.

Before he could catch up again, her lips left his, trailed down his neck and over his chest. She sank downwards, her hands drifting over his body as she kissed lower, as she swirled her tongue around his navel and dropped to her knees before him.

August swallowed hard.

She trailed kisses along the waistband of his jeans.

He might have made a valiant effort to claw back some nobility and stop her at that point, but the fire in her eyes dared him to try it, and promised he would regret it.

They held his as she made fast work of his jeans, popping the first button and then gripping the two sides to pull them apart in one swift stroke. Cool air washed over his cock and he groaned, swallowed hard and tried to keep his head.

Maya made that impossible when she lowered hers, still holding his gaze captive with hers, and slowly ran her tongue up the length of his cock from root to tip.

He bit his lip, tipped his head back and pressed it hard into the wall.

Dear-fucking-gods.

She moaned and licked him again, not even the slightest tremble in her as she gripped his hips and held him fast, stopping him from moving. He wasn't sure he could have even if he had wanted to move. He was ninety-nine percent certain he had already left his body and was just floating above it, watching as she went to war on him.

She was killing him.

Her soft warm tongue pressed into the ridge on the underside of his cock, sending tingles shooting down to his balls, and he groaned and pressed harder against the wall, fought to keep standing as his knees weakened again.

She loosed another moan and feathered kisses up the length of him to the tip. He grunted as she took him in her hand and pushed downwards, revealing the blunt crown. Oh gods. He wasn't sure he could handle this after all.

She moved her hand up and down, stroking his shaft, ripping moan after moan from him that she seemed to enjoy as she studied his cock. He barked out a groan when she lowered her hand to cup his balls, earning a startled gasp from her. Her surprise at his reaction lasted all of a second, a brief reprieve that didn't give him enough time to pull his shit together before she discovered how to completely undo him.

Maya rolled his balls in her hand as she licked the head of his cock, fluttering her tongue over it and teasing the slit.

"Fuck."

She blinked up at him, a hint of colour on her cheeks.

Shocked that she had made him swear like that with only a touch?

He wasn't. Hell, he was holding back. He wanted to unleash every fucking swear word in the dictionary, and some made up ones, on her, in every fucking language he knew.

His knees almost buckled when she wrapped her lips around him, her hand still working magic on his sac.

"Sweet fucking gods almighty." He shook as she took him into her mouth. It was moist. Hot. Too fucking good.

He snapped.

His left hand shot to her black hair, twisting it into his fist, and he grunted as he shallowly thrust into her warm mouth, struggling for control, aware he was probably scaring the shit out of her.

She moaned.

Actually fucking moaned.

The vibrations of it ran down from the head of his cock to his balls, which instantly tightened.

"Oh fuck," he breathed and pushed her back.

He gripped his cock, held it so tight it killed like a motherfucker, stopping himself from climaxing.

August breathed hard.

As his body began to relax, the urge to spill fading, he grew painfully aware of Maya's eyes on him.

And how he was standing over her with a death grip on his cock with one hand and her hair with the other.

"I was… ah…" He looked down at his hand on his length and tried to convince himself to release it, but for some damned reason he just ended up standing there, still holding it like he was about to jack off and spill on her face. "I didn't want to…"

He wasn't sure whether he was saying he didn't want to climax on her face, or hadn't wanted to climax at all.

Maybe it was both.

Maya blinked.

Her amber eyes dropped to his cock and the damn thing jerked in response.

"It was a bit too good." Gods, he sounded like the virgin now.

He had talked dirty to countless females, had been blunt and an adult about things, saying shit straight.

It didn't feel right to do that with Maya though.

She had him tied in knots, wanting to do everything right. Perfect.

"Oh," she said, raising her eyes to his again.

A flicker of understanding shone in them.

She reached up and took his hand from her hair. He wasn't sure what she was going to do when she released it.

His breath left him in another dizzying rush when she wrapped her hand around his on his cock and began moving it slowly, just enough to keep him painfully hard, and her eyes met his.

"I'll stop when you say. I just want to make you feel good, like you made me feel good."

She leaned in and undid him all over again, wrapping her lips around his flesh as she moved his own hand on his cock.

"Gods, Maya, just looking at you makes me feel good." He cringed when he realised he was sounding like a complete pervert again.

He hadn't meant looking at her while she sucked on his cock. He had meant looking at her anytime, when she was doing anything.

Which was one hell of a fucking revelation.

It knocked him sideways so hard he almost missed the massive cue his body threw at him.

He pushed Maya back the second it registered, breathing hard as he struggled to tamp down the need rushing through him, threatening to catapult him over the edge.

Maya gazed up at him, a touch of innocence in her eyes as she watched him, but mixed with a hell of a lot of wickedness.

Wickedness she certainly seemed to be embracing.

She rose to her feet, clamped her hands over his shoulders, and kissed him hard.

August groaned and lost himself in it, in the way her tongue met his and teased his fangs, sending hot shivers dancing over the skin she seared with her light touch, stroking her hands over his shoulders and down his chest.

"I want you."

Those whispered words were his undoing.

He shot past the point of no return in a heartbeat, left it so far behind he couldn't even see it in the distance, and caught her around the waist, lifting her at the same time as he turned with her to pin her back against the wall.

She moaned and kissed him harder, hooked her right hand around his neck and tugged him closer. He groaned as her legs looped around his waist, the skirt of her dress falling away to allow his aching shaft to press against her slick heat. A little whimper left her lips and she trembled as she tentatively rubbed against him.

Damn. He wouldn't last five seconds if she did that.

The need to be inside her, to fill her up and satisfy her every desire, was too strong, driving him to obey it. He clutched her bare backside in his left hand, groaned and shuddered as her moistness coated his fingers and she whimpered again, rubbed him harder, a desperate edge to her actions and the feelings that echoed inside him.

She needed him.

Gods, he needed her too.

He seized his cock with his free hand, slowly lifted her with his other one and eased it down through her folds, drinking in her gasps and moans as he rubbed her with the blunt head. When he reached her core, she stilled, breathing hard, and he focused on her, trying to pick out her feelings, needing to know what they were as they stood on the precipice.

No fear.

There was only excitement, arousal, need that matched his own.

She really wanted this.

He eased his hips forwards, pushing slowly into her, a monumental achievement considering his every instinct was screaming at him to claim her, to make her his.

She moaned and breathed harder, her breath washing across his lips in sharp bursts as she tried to keep kissing him. He kissed her gently, giving her something to focus on as he inched deeper.

Gods, she was tight. Hot. Fucking incredible.

He breathed harder too, fighting to hold himself back and deny the urge to spill before he had even started to make this good for her.

"August," she whispered against his lips, and he had never heard his name said so sweetly, with so much need.

Shock blasted through him when she moved in his arms, pushing him deeper inside her far quicker than he had intended.

He stilled, afraid he had hurt her.

Her moan was ambrosia to his ears, soothed his soul and eased his heart.

He held her on his cock and breathed hard to cope with the onslaught of feeling that being inside her stirred in him. He hadn't been prepared for it, hadn't expected to feel so moved by just being inside her, so content and so lost for words.

What was it about Maya that made her so different to every female he had ever known?

What was it about Maya that made her feel like home?

As if he had never truly known the meaning of that word until she had walked into his life?

He shut out the thought that came next, not wanting to contemplate it, because it wasn't going to happen. She had told him this was a moment of madness, a wild fling before she left him forever, walked right back out of his life.

This was all they could have.

No matter how many times he told himself that, he couldn't make it sink in. Something soul-deep rebelled against it, roared that it didn't have to be this way, even when he knew that it did.

He couldn't take a mate from a different species.

Not even when that mate was as beautiful as Maya.

He needed to find his fated one and set an example.

Even if it killed him.

He wasn't sure anyone else could ever make him feel the way Maya did.

Her lips sought his, brushed sweetly across them and pulled him back to her, an anchor in the violent storm of his emotions. He growled and kissed her hard, couldn't help himself as he cursed the gods, cursed his ancestors and every fucking power that had made Maya and had put her on his path.

If he couldn't have her forever, he would at least have her for now.

He swallowed her gasp as he eased out of her and back in, setting a slow tempo that felt too good, brought light back into his soul and chased the shadows away, narrowing the world back down to only them.

She softened the kiss as he thrust long and slow into her, a moan leaving her lips each time their bodies met. He drank down each one, drowning in her and the light that seared his soul, grew brighter with each passing moment, bathing him in warmth.

What was it about Maya that made him feel this way?

August pulled back and stared into her dazzling amber eyes, seeking the answer to that question in them.

Gods she was beautiful.

She stared right back at him, her rosy lips parted on her moans as he took them higher, her hands clutching his shoulders, clinging to him as he clung to her.

"August," she husked, and ripped a groan from him as she started to move, countering his thrusts, driving her body down onto his cock as he thrust back inside her.

He kept watching her, memorising every emotion that danced across her beautiful face and shone in her eyes as he sent her higher, quickening his pace just enough to have her eyebrows furrowing and her head tipping back, and her nails pressing into his bare shoulders.

He wasn't sure he had ever made love to anyone.

Maya was his first.

And gods, he wanted her to be his only.

He wanted to be her only.

He leaned in and pressed his forehead against hers, overcome as that thought, that burning need ricocheted through him.

Maya's palm came to rest on his cheek, gentle and soft, her touch filled with understanding and telling him that she could feel him, could feel the conflict and the confusion, and the damned feelings she had awoken in his heart.

She stroked her fingers along his jaw, tipped his head up and caught his lips in a soft kiss.

Damn it.

He growled and kissed her, tried to wash away everything that was dragging him down and forget it all.

She moaned and wrapped her arms around his neck, pulling him closer, her kiss turning fierce, helping him shove all the messy shit out of his head. He swallowed her gasp as he clutched her backside in both hands and drove deeper, faster, until her heart and his thundered in his ears and she started to rock against him, her body flexing around his cock.

Her need spiked.

He felt it the moment it did, the second she reached the pinnacle and was close.

He kissed her deeper, meeting her desperate thrusts, weathering the storm as she clawed at his shoulders and locked her feet behind his bottom, using them to force him harder into her.

August curled his hips, driving as deep as he could go.

Maya tensed.

He covered her mouth with his and kissed her, muffling her cries as she shattered, her body quivering around his cock and her nails pressing so hard into his shoulders he could smell the tinny scent of blood.

He groaned and followed her, grunted with each throb of his cock as he spilled inside her, claiming her in the only way he could. She trembled with each pulse of his length, whimpered whenever her body echoed one, an aftershock of pleasure rolling through her.

Sweet gods.

When he had finally caught his breath, he swept his lips across hers.

She didn't respond.

August pulled back, a ripple of fear racing through him to leave him cold.

Maya stared at him through wide eyes, tears lining her lashes.

He stumbled backwards when she shoved him, pushing him away and landing on her feet.

"Maya…"

She refused to look at him.

He reached for her, aching with a need to hold her and find out what was wrong, to comfort her because she was hurting, but she smacked his hand away.

The cold feeling spread, icy fingers reaching towards his heart.

She rubbed her tears away, sniffed and lifted her head, her black hair falling around her shoulders.

Her eyes met his.

No trace of feeling in them.

"This was fun… but it was all we can have… just this stolen moment with each other."

She was gone before he could respond, leaving him reeling in the booth as the curtain swayed to his right, staring at the black wall where she had been.

That cold filled the hollow space in his chest where his heart had been.

A heart she had stolen.

CHAPTER 10

Maya cursed herself as she ran through the heaving nightclub, tears streaming down her face. She had been an idiot to think she could have a moment with August and not regret it, not feel affected by it.

It had been too wonderful.

He had been too wonderful.

She shoved through a group of demon males, not slowing when they growled at her and shouted, probably calling her names in their tongue.

She didn't care.

All that mattered was running, putting as much distance as she could between her and August.

She couldn't bear it.

It tore her apart inside, ripped her in two directions until she wavered between the male she was running from and the one she was running towards.

She reached the door to the backroom of Underworld and punched in the code Sherry had given her on the silver panel beside it.

The moment it clicked, she twisted the handle and pushed inside, slamming the door behind her.

She didn't slow.

She ran up the stairs on the left side of the room, taking them as quickly as she could manage and battling an urge to shift so she could move faster.

Fear began to seep into her heart, fear of what her future held.

She hit the corridor on the second floor and kept running, not stopping until she reached the door of her room.

She opened it, turned and shut it, and stood there with her hand clutching the knob, her breath coming so fast she feared she might pass out.

She had to go.

Byron and the pride were depending on her to do this.

It didn't matter how miserable she was going to be now, how she was going to spend the rest of her life thinking about August.

Thinking about what might have been.

She screamed and pummelled the door with her fists, fury and fear colliding inside her, mingling with the pain that tore through her, born of her heart.

Gods, why had the fates brought her to August?

It was just too cruel.

She sagged to her knees and pressed her hands to the door, her head hanging between them.

She wasn't strong enough to choose him over her brother, over her pride.

Over the wishes of her parents.

She needed to honour them, needed to put her pride first and her brother's safety before the desires of her heart.

But why did it have to hurt so much?

She pressed one hand to her chest and closed her fingers over it, digging her nails into her skin.

Why did it feel as if she might die if she never saw August again?

"Fuck," she hissed and banged her fist against the door. "Fuck. Fuck!"

Awareness prickled down her spine.

He was coming.

If she saw him again, she wouldn't be strong enough to resist him, wouldn't be strong enough to go through with her family's plans for her.

She shot to her feet, grabbed her bag from the end of her bed and shoved all her belongings into it, leaving only a pair of cream knickers out on the bed. When her bag was packed, she grabbed those and hurried into the bathroom.

Her hands shook as she cleaned herself up, heart pounding in her ears.

Someone knocked at the door.

Her heart stopped.

"Maya."

Her breath rushed from her.

Grey.

She tugged her knickers on and then ran to the door and opened it. His pale blue eyes darted down to her, and darkened.

"You've been crying," he said, his silvery eyebrows dipping low, hardening his features until he looked every bit the warrior he was, ready to kill someone.

She shook her head. "I need to go."

"Is it that snow leopard?"

"Please, Grey," she snapped, and he blinked, shock dancing across his face. She had never raised her voice at him before. She lowered it to a whisper. "Please… I want to leave… now."

"Maya," he started.

"Now," she cut him off, her eyebrows furrowing as her heart stung with the thought of seeing August again.

She wanted him, more than anything, more than life itself, but she had to do this. She had to do what others wanted for her, and place the pride and her family first.

"Please?"

Grey's handsome face hardened and he pushed past her, and for a moment she thought he was going to argue with her, was going to give August a chance to find her.

He picked up her bag and her coat, grabbed her hand and walked out into the corridor, not looking back at her. "Come on."

Maya followed him to his room next to hers, and waited as he gathered his bag and his own jacket. She put her coat on, her hands still trembling, heart refusing to steady.

Grey slung both of their bags over his shoulder, seized her hand again, and tugged her back out into the hall.

She trailed behind him, her eyes fixed on the back of his black jacket as it stretched across his broad shoulders, her heart aching and tears threatening to line her lashes.

She could feel Grey's hurt, his desire to stop her from doing this.

It echoed inside her, burned as fiercely as August's pain, and her own.

She didn't want to hurt her brother, but she needed to do this now, before the strength she had mustered gave way and she placed everyone at risk.

She hadn't meant to hurt August either.

But she had.

Gods, she had.

She could feel it beating in her chest as Grey led her down to the ground floor and out of the emergency exit, into an alley behind Underworld.

She could feel it as he hailed a taxi and loaded her into the back.

She could feel it as the vehicle pulled away, taking her far from him.

It continued to echo in her even then, even with miles separating them, and she knew this pain would always be there, etched on her soul forever.

A reminder that she had paid the ultimate price for her pride.

For her brothers.

She had sacrificed herself.

CHAPTER 11

Maya clouded August's every moment, whether he was awake or asleep. He couldn't focus on anything but the tigress. He kept seeing her wherever he went, kept dreaming about her.

She haunted him.

He wasn't sure he would ever be the same again, would ever be able to settle and find peace. A restless feeling gnawed at him every second, had his snow leopard side pacing, and had him wandering the mountains alone, lost in thought, drawn to places he was unfamiliar with.

Places that were dangerous.

He would have walked right into a crevasse that morning if Dalton hadn't found him at that moment and pulled him back, shaking him back to reality.

He couldn't remember walking up the valley between the two snowy peaks that loomed above the village, had no recollection of how he had gotten there. A feeling had lingered though, a sensation that he needed to go that way, that his life depended on it.

Gods. He was losing his mind.

Dalton had kept a close watch on him all day, not moving more than a foot from his side, his pale golden eyes wary.

August scrubbed a hand over his red hair and then replaced the black knit skullcap. He kicked at the fresh layer of snow that covered the plateau, watching the fine white dust catch the wind and dance into the forested valley far below.

Normally, he found the view of the white capped peaks that rose high above the forest and river breathtaking, the contrast between the green of the trees, the pure white of the snow and the deep blue sky something beautiful to behold.

Now it lacked colour.

It lacked the life it had once had.

He sighed, his breath fogging in the cold thin air.

Dalton shifted foot to foot beside him, stamping them to keep the chill off.

They were snow leopards, but they still felt the cold, the climate up in their secluded mountain home a little too frigid for their warm blood. It was necessary though. The pride had to be protected, and to do that, they had made sacrifices, cutting themselves off from the world below.

Talon's words rang in his head.

Maya was doing the same damn thing.

She had chosen to make a sacrifice for the sake of her pride.

Her brother had been frantic when August had finally pieced himself together enough to leave the booth and go after Maya. Grey had already taken her away, and neither of them had stopped to say goodbye to Talon. They had disappeared without a word.

Because of him.

Maya had run away from him.

She had run straight to another alpha, one who didn't deserve her but one she was promised to according to Talon.

Was she there now?

With another male?

He threw his head back and roared.

The sound echoed around the mountains, mocked him with the impotent fury in it and all the pain.

Pain he felt sure was never going to leave him.

"August," Dalton said in a low voice, a note of caution in it.

He nodded, knew that it was no use and yelling about it so the world knew his pain wasn't going to change anything. The pride were already talking, had noticed he had returned from London a different male, and he could understand their concerns but they had nothing to worry about. He was still their alpha.

He was still going to do his best for the sake of the pride.

"They're here."

He glanced at Dalton, who jerked his stubbly chin towards the right side of the plateau, where it gently sloped down towards the forest below.

August looked there and spotted three figures clad in brightly coloured thick jackets and trousers steadily making their way along the path that followed the base of the jagged peak to his right.

The alpha from their nearest neighbouring pride and two others.

The male led, far larger than the two who followed him.

August tracked them as he walked towards that side of the village, heading across the open land that bordered the sheer drop into the valley, a space they used for social gatherings. To his right, the small houses of the village clustered together, their deep stone foundations dark against the snow. At several of the two room houses, females dressed in warm protective clothing stood on the stone steps that led up to the main part of the structure, sweeping snow off them. Some of the owners had chosen to decorate the white panels set into the thick dark wooden beams of the houses, painting them in brightly coloured scenes and patterns.

Snow slid from the low sloping roof of one of the houses as he passed, and the children playing beneath it squealed and burst into a fit of giggles as it landed on them.

Gods, he wished he was that age again, free of the worries of the world that rested on his shoulders.

He stopped at the edge of the village and did his best to keep his eyes on the three figures coming towards him now and off the end of the valley they crossed, away from the point where the two peaks met.

The urge to keep walking was strong, almost overpowering him as it filled him with a need to go to that point, and to not stop when he reached it, to keep walking until he was home.

He *was* home.

August looked over his shoulder at the village, at his pride. This was his home.

His heart whispered that it wasn't, not anymore. He had found his home in a beautiful tigress.

The alpha reached him and he pushed her out of his thoughts and turned to the male.

The male pulled the burnt orange scarf that covered his mouth and nose down, revealing a face worn and lined and touched with warmth. That light reached the male's dark gold eyes as he smiled and extended a hand.

"August?"

August took it, their thick gloves making it hard to do anything more than loosely grip each other's hands as they shook. "Luis."

The male beamed at him, his accent tinged with a French edge. "The very same. The journey was long, and a little cold for my liking. Sixty years in the mountains and I am still not used to the climate."

"My home is warm, and you are welcome," August said and glanced at the two who accompanied the old snow leopard alpha.

Females.

Both were young, probably hadn't seen their one hundredth year.

He left their care to Dalton and swept his hand out to his left, pointing the way to his home and ushering Luis towards it.

"Your journey was good?" August said, trying to remember all the small talk Cavanaugh had taught him was part of the process of meeting with another pride and trying to shut out how thinking about Cavanaugh now made him think about Maya too.

Luis nodded. "As good as can be expected. The final leg was a little rough on me. I think I am finally getting too old for this."

"I am sure that is not the case at all." Although August had sent three males armed with climbing ropes and gear down to the sheer cliff that provided the only access to the pride village.

Rather than asking Luis to scale the cliff face, he had given the alpha a lift, the males pulling him and his entourage up on the ropes.

August was ashamed to admit he hadn't even thought about doing such a thing before Cavanaugh had mentioned it.

Gods, he could just imagine the ageing alpha losing his footing during the climb and plummeting to his death.

Would have been just August's fucking luck too.

The entire snow leopard community would have come down on his head.

He held the door to his home open.

As alpha, he had a little more space than the other houses. Rather than there only being a living space on the ground floor, and steep steps up to a single bedroom on the upper floor, he had a living space with a large open fire on the left as he entered, surrounded by two armchairs and a couch, and a small kitchen opposite the main door, and off to his right was another door that led into a bathroom. On the first floor, there were two bedrooms off a narrow corridor.

It was a mansion in snow leopard terms.

The alpha nodded his head in approval and stripped off his bright orange coat, hanging it by the door. He kicked off his boots, and his thermal waterproof trousers followed, revealing a loose pair of dark grey trekking trousers.

August followed suit, ditching his black trousers and red jacket, and his hat and scarf. He tossed his gloves on the coffee table as Luis sat down on the armchair facing the door. The male sighed and sagged into the soft chair.

"By the gods, this feels good." Luis smiled at him. "Daughters."

The two females removed their outdoor clothing at the door, leaving it on the pile with their father's, and joined him, sitting on the couch close to him. The taller one, a brunette with silver-gold eyes, sat closest to Luis, her navy jeans and red roll neck sweater a contrast against his dark brown couch. Her sister, a younger female with sandy hair and gold eyes that matched her father's, sat beside her, dressed in similar jeans but a blue sweater.

Dalton closed the door. "I'll make some tea."

"Make that something warm with a little heat." Luis grinned. "If you catch my meaning."

August did, and the smile that spread across Dalton's face and lit up his pale golden eyes said he did too. He disappeared into the kitchen.

It was far too early in the day to be drinking, but Cavanaugh had warned him it might be the case. Quite often, trade negotiations were fuelled by their local brew, a sweet strong alcohol served hot to keep the chill off.

August was surprised any negotiating took place at all.

Apparently, sometimes it didn't.

Sometimes alphas just ended up visiting each other to get drunk and speak with another alpha about everything that was on their mind, all the things they couldn't really discuss with anyone at their own pride and only an alpha would understand.

August could see the appeal in that.

He looked over his left shoulder, seeing beyond the wall of his home to that enticing dip between the two peaks.

"Do you have somewhere you need to be?" Luis said.

August quickly turned to face him and shook his head, just as Dalton walked in. He caught the look on his friend's face and frowned at him, warning him not to say a damn word. He was fine.

Dalton set a mug down in front of him, and one down in front of Luis, and went back to the kitchen, running his hand over his long silver-gold hair in a way that screamed of frustration.

It had been a mistake to tell Dalton about Maya.

His friend had tried to convince him to go after her, even when August had told him that it was impossible, and not only because she was promised to another. He had to do right by the pride, and picking a tigress over finding his fated one was the opposite of that.

As much as he hated the traditions of their kind, he had to abide by them. One day, he would change them and bring his kin into the modern age, freeing them of the shackles of society's demands, allowing them to choose who they loved and who they wanted as their mate without fear of being condemned by others in their pride.

Most of the pride weren't ready for such a bold move though, and were unlikely to tolerate it from an alpha who had only held the position for five months.

Gods, it wasn't right though.

Cavanaugh was proof of that. Years ago, his cousin had taken a beating from Stellan on purpose, had let the male defeat him and snatch the pride from his hands because the position of alpha had stood between him and claiming the female he loved—his fated mate, Eloise.

It had plunged the pride into turmoil and into dark times. Stellan had been cruel, a tyrant, abusive and vicious, and his reign had been hard on the pride. It had shaken them all.

In the end, Cavanaugh had set them free of Stellan's rule, and August had taken on the mantle of alpha to free his cousin, because even though he had saved them, even though they had witnessed what tradition had done and how it had forced Cavanaugh to place them all in danger just so he could be with Eloise in the way his heart needed him to be, the pride would still have demanded Cavanaugh mate with a highborn female and take Eloise as a mistress.

So as much as he wanted to tear down some traditions and build new ones in their place, he had to wait.

The pride were barely on their feet again, slowly recovering from Stellan's rule. Trying to force such a dramatic change to their traditions on them would be too much.

But gods, he wanted to do it.

He wanted to stand out there on that plateau and roar that it wasn't right, that everyone should be free to choose who they loved without repercussions.

He wanted to roar that as of that moment, they were all free. The lowborn free to love the highborn.

A snow leopard free to love a tigress.

Dalton returned with tea for the females, stopping in the doorway to the kitchen, concern flickering across his face as he looked at August.

August lowered his head, closed his eyes and pinched the bridge of his nose.

Gods, when had he started losing his grip on reality? When had a fantasy become more appealing than it?

He hung his head lower. When Maya had run off with his heart.

If it wouldn't drag Cavanaugh back to the pride and jeopardise his relationship with Eloise, August would walk right out the door and abdicate his position as alpha right that moment.

He would break the shackles that bound him so he could be with Maya.

"August is tired from his trip to see his cousin in London." Dalton's deep voice rolled through the room, rich and warm, comforting him as much as his friend's hand did as it came down on his right shoulder, gripping it gently. "I imagine you are just as tired from your long journey."

"As deep as my bones… but the drink is taking care of warming those." Luis lifted his cup as August raised his head and opened his eyes, looking across the table at the male.

He grabbed his own mug and lifted it too, saluting the male and dragging himself out of the mire of his thoughts. They were pointless. Maya didn't want to be with him. She had made her choice.

"There is nothing good brew cannot fix." He took a deep draught of the hot drink.

Luis grinned at him.

Fuck, those words had sounded hollow to him. His heart roared that there was something good brew couldn't fix.

The gulf that lay between him and where he wanted to be.

Between him and Maya.

He did his best to listen as Dalton drew up a chair beside him and Luis talked to him of his pride. He made small talk like a fucking pro, using all of Cavanaugh's pointers, discussing everything from the recent changes in land rights between mortals down in the valleys to the latest curriculum he was trying to implement in the small school at the centre of his pride village.

But all the while, part of his mind was thinking about that dip between the peaks and what lay beyond it.

Maya.

The day wore on, and three more mugs of brew came and went, and his head finally grew fuzzy enough at the edges that he stopped thinking about a certain tigress.

For at least five seconds.

"I suppose we should discuss one final matter… the offer of one of my daughters as a female for you."

"I'm honoured, but no." Those words had left August's lips before he had even thought about answering Luis's offer.

Luis's sandy eyebrows rose, intrigued brightening his eyes. "You already have a mate?"

August thought hard about that, and started to get the feeling that maybe he did.

Maybe the reason he couldn't get Maya out of his head, the reason he felt drawn to that place beyond the mountains, and the reason he had been overcome with new, raw and intense feelings when they had been together was because she was more than just another female.

She was something to him.

Something that was impossible.

He was starting to think that she had been lying to protect him, and to protect herself, when she had told him that he couldn't be her fated one.

Something Talon had said when he had been leaving Underworld, something that had sounded flippant and unimportant at the time, slammed back into his head with a force that shook him.

Maya could be a little hellcat at times.

August had taken that to mean she had her wild moments, when she was out of control, like the gym and their time in the booth.

What if Talon had been trying to tell him something?

Shit, now that he was thinking about it, Cavanaugh had spoken about the female bartender, Sherry, as if she was mortal all the times he had talked to his cousin via the satellite phone.

August had met her during his stay at Underworld.

Sherry was a tiger shifter, mated to Talon.

If she had been mortal, then Talon had turned her. Impossible. Unless. There was one species of feline shifter that could turn mortals.

Hellcats.

He caught a flash of Maya looking at him in the booth.

A flare of blue around her pupils.

A shiver chased over his arms and down his thighs.

If Maya's family had hellcat blood, it changed all the rules.

Hellcats could find their mate with any species.

Even the ones who could only find it within their own.

Ones like his.

Gods.

He shot to his feet, ripping a startled gasp from the two females to his right.

Maya was his fated one.

He was a fucking blind idiot.

He had been so convinced that she couldn't be that he had ignored all the tell-tale signs that should have alerted him to the fact he had found his fated mate.

And he had let her slip through his hands.

Fuck having only a stolen moment with her.

Fuck traditions too.

The pride could damn well accept the change he was about to make, because he was done with seeing tradition bind people and stand between them and what they wanted—who they loved.

It ended now.

He was dragging his pride into the modern age whether they liked it or not. For his sake. For the sake of Dalton. For every male or female in his pride who loved someone different in status to them. He was doing this.

Cavanaugh was sure to have a few words to say about it, and the correct behaviour of an alpha, but August didn't care. He wasn't his cousin. He hadn't been raised to obey outdated traditions and moulded into an alpha from birth, shaped into a male who would rather bend for the sake of the pride than break down whatever stood between him and what was right.

August had been raised to be a fighter, a warrior capable of defending the pride, a male who would rather break down the barriers.

His cousin was strong, but he had been weak where tradition was concerned, had let it come between him and Eloise, when he should have roared a massive 'fuck you' at it like August was going to do.

He was alpha now. He had the power to do this, to set everyone free, himself included.

He was going to do it.

Cavanaugh had been right about one thing though—he had fought for what he wanted.

August was going to take a leaf out of his book.

He was going to fight for Maya.

But to do that, he was going to need some help.

He had just the tiger for the job.

CHAPTER 12

The journey had been long, and far more than just physically tiring for Maya. She trudged the path through the dense forest, following on Grey's heels, her heart still aching in her chest as fear slowly built inside her, fear that the male she was about to meet would be as bad as Talon had heard.

Gods, she felt awful for leaving Underworld without saying goodbye to her brother.

The need to run before she had a chance to change her mind had been at the helm, driving her away from him and away from August.

She missed them both.

She had only known August a short time, but he had carved out a part of her heart for himself, and that part ached fiercer than the rest, blazed with fire that wouldn't abate. She feared it would burn forever, never giving her peace, always reminding her of what she had done.

Grey glanced back at her, concern and warmth in his blue eyes. The sunlight filtering through the trees played across his silver hair and over the shoulders of his black coat. He adjusted the bags on his shoulder, sighed and faced forwards again.

"It's still not too late to turn back," he said, quietly enough that she knew he was warring with himself again, torn in two just as she was.

He didn't want her here, didn't want to hand her over to the Altay pride's alpha, Pyotr, and definitely didn't want to leave without her.

Doubt trickled into her heart and her steps slowed.

Grey turned to face her. "You don't have to do this, Maya."

She didn't.

She glanced over her shoulder.

She could turn back right now and run far from this place, run to where her heart wanted to be.

She clenched her fists at her sides.

She couldn't.

Pyotr was expecting her, and if she didn't show up, he would send males to her pride to bring her to him. When they found she wasn't there, those males would attack her kin, and they would hurt Byron.

Grey's hand came down on her shoulder, a touch that took her back to the streets of London, before she had met August, before her heart had been thrown into turmoil, torn between two males.

Byron hurt her at times, but he was trying to do what was best for the pride.

She had to do her best too.

She lifted her gloved hand and placed it over Grey's on her shoulder, and raised her eyes to meet his blue ones. Gods, she was going to miss him most out of all her brothers. He had been her best friend for decades, her shoulder to cry on and her staunch protector.

Who was going to be that for her now?

She looked beyond him, to the distance where the trees thinned and smoke curled lazily into the air above their branches.

She knew no one in that village, not even the male she was meant to wed.

She would be alone.

She was sure her parents hadn't meant for things to happen this way, that they had planned for Pyotr to visit her with his family, and for her to visit his pride, before anything happened between them.

But both her parents and his were dead, gone, and whatever plans they'd had were gone with them.

She wished she had the courage to turn away, to treat this contract in the way Talon and Grey wanted her to, as if the deaths of their parents had made it null and void.

Perhaps it took greater courage to keep walking forwards, to go through with the promise they had made, stepping into the unknown for the sake of her pride and her brothers.

Courage that she had.

She took Grey's hand from her shoulder, squeezed it, and then walked past him, continuing towards the village.

Her steps faltered again.

Was she making a terrible mistake?

She turned to Grey.

Her eyes widened.

"Brother." She reached for him, but he moved in the blink of an eye, pivoting away from her and seizing her wrist, tugging her close to his back.

The three tigers growled and snapped their fangs at him as they eased out of the undergrowth, moving to surround her and Grey.

Instinct roared to the fore, the need to fight blazing to life inside her to burn away her control, and she bared her fangs at the tiger nearest her as he prowled closer.

Grey growled and let the bags drop from his shoulders.

Clothed as he was in a thick jumper and jacket, and his jeans and boots, performing a shift before the males attacked him would be impossible.

She didn't stand a much better chance in her thick leggings and dress, and the knee-length coat she wore over the top.

Both of them were strong in their human form, their hellcat genes meaning they could match the strength of the tigers, but they would be vulnerable. Three on two were bad odds, and the tigers' claws and fangs would give them the edge.

Grey moved closer to her and whispered, "Run when I say."

"No." She couldn't leave him.

Wouldn't.

He was strong, agile, an experienced fighter, but even he had his limits. Three on one were impossible odds for him. He looked over his shoulder at her, something shining in his blue eyes that tore a cry from her throat and had her shaking her head.

She wasn't going to let him sacrifice himself so she could survive.

She stepped past him before he could stop her, intending to launch herself at the tiger in the middle of the group.

A male voice thick with a Russian accent stopped her cold.

"You intend to attack my bride?"

A chill went through her.

Pyotr.

The three tigers lowered their heads and backed away, disappearing one by one into the scrub. Footsteps sounded behind her and she felt Grey tense, but she couldn't convince her body to move as her nerves raged out of control, fear of seeing her intended mate for the first time freezing her feet to the forest floor.

The male said something in Russian.

Cold slithered down her spine.

She was his beloved.

He would never be hers.

She would never love him.

Because she was in love with another.

Her fated male.

Maya turned on her heel to face Pyotr, felt nothing as she looked into his golden eyes and his broad mouth curled into a warm smile.

He was handsome, with tousled short hair that matched the colour of his eyes, and a tall broad frame, but he did nothing for her.

Her heart called for another male, one with red hair and pure silver eyes, one who had awakened her soul and brought her to life.

She forced herself to bow her head to him though, to show him the courtesy and respect he would expect from her. That was all he would ever have from her—only as much as was necessary and expected.

"Maya," Pyotr said, his tone light, almost playful. "You do not need to be so meek around me."

If that was meant as an invitation to be wicked, to be wild, she was going to have to turn him down. She had no intention of being anything like that with him. Soon, it would be his right to claim her as his mate, but all he would touch was her body. He would never touch her soul. He would never reach her heart.

"Come, come." He beckoned her, and she went to him, didn't stop him when he placed his arm around her shoulders and led her towards the village in the distance. "It is lucky I came upon you when I did, no? My warriors are a little... agitated... they crave a fight I cannot give them now."

Her blood chilled another five degrees as she caught the meaning in his words.

He had stirred his males up with a need to fight in preparation for sending them to her pride if she didn't show, and she had disappointed them by appearing as promised.

How long would he have given her before he had sent his males to attack her kin?

She looked up at his profile, trying to see the male Talon had painted him to be. Was he really a vicious bastard? As cruel as the rumours said?

He turned a dazzling smile on her.

"Do you like what you see?" His smile widened, his golden eyes gaining a spark she didn't like as his pupils dilated and she sensed he wanted to look her over, wanted to take in her body and see what the pact with her pride had gotten him.

She didn't nod.

She averted her eyes, because if she had kept looking at him, he would have seen the loathing in her, the disgust and the desire to leave him.

"You will warm to me soon enough." He patted her shoulder.

Grey growled quietly from behind her.

Pyotr looked back at him. "You are welcome to stay until the ceremony is complete."

She could just picture the look Grey would give him in response to that. Her brother wasn't very good at hiding his feelings. He had a habit of showing it all on his face.

Pyotr's smile held as he shifted his golden gaze down to her again. "Your brother is not very talkative."

She managed a small smile and tried to sound light and cheerful. "It has been a long journey and I'm afraid both of us are not in good spirits."

"Ah." He nodded. "Of course. It is a long trek to the pride. I am sorry we do not have a road to our pride, as you do near yours. Relocating to that small reserve in South Wales must have been difficult for you all."

Her blood chilled further.

How did he know where her pride were?

Byron had sent word to him about sending her before the pride had left the old village at Tèarmann in Scotland, before her brother had even decided upon where their next home would be located.

She masked her shock, not wanting to give him the satisfaction of seeing it. He was making a statement, making it clear that he knew where Byron and her pride were, and that his warriors were ready to go there. All he had to do was say the word.

He was threatening her.

Grey growled again, and she wanted to echo him.

They entered the boundary of the village, a gathering of small single storey cabins that all faced each other in a wide circle, with a larger one directly in front of her. Pyotr's cabin. Her skin crawled at the thought of living there.

The three tigers who had threatened her and Grey slunk out of the undergrowth on either side of her and she frowned at the one on her left as he shifted back, transforming into a huge male with jet black hair and near-black eyes.

They had been stalking her and Grey, keeping watch over their alpha, ready to attack if either her or her brother attempted to hurt him.

The other two shifted back and the three walked off together, naked and unabashed, strolling through the village towards the centre where a huge fire blazed.

Shock danced through her as she looked there.

Other males walked around naked, chatting and laughing, sharing a drink. There were two more off by one of the cabins too, sharpening knives on a whetstone.

What kind of pride was this?

The most modest it got was a male who was wearing an apron while he crouched in front of the fire, cooking something.

She looked at Pyotr.

He casually shrugged. "My warriors prefer the freedom to shift."

From where she was standing, it looked more like his warriors enjoyed walking around naked in front of the females who moved around the small village.

Females who were few in number.

She counted only three.

Were there more in the buildings?

At least the three she could see were clothed, although they all wore the same drab grey dress with a white pinafore tied over it.

"Come. I will show you to your temporary quarters." He beckoned one of the females, and the brunette obediently came to him, her head bowed the whole time. "Take the male to his cabin."

"I'll stay with Maya," Grey said, but Pyotr ignored him and led her away as the female tugged on Grey's arm, trying to pull him in the other direction.

The males watched Maya as she walked through the village, their eyes drilling into her. She kept her eyes off them, not interested in seeing them naked and getting the feeling that some of them wanted her to look at them. Several of them stood as she approached, their hands settling on their hips, trying to draw her focus there.

Pyotr growled at one, and the blond cast him a black look before he moved away, returning to speaking with another male.

Why had Pyotr felt the need to challenge the male and warn him away?

He was alpha, a position the male should have respected, and as far as she knew the entire pride were aware she was here to become his bride.

She looked back at the male, curiosity sparking to life inside her, but Pyotr moved, blocking her view with his chest, and growled at her.

He pushed her forwards, and she stumbled over some wooden steps and almost hit the door of the cabin.

"I am sorry," he muttered, that smile back on his face when she risked a glance at him, and gently righted her. He raked his eyes over her, concern warming them. "You are not hurt?"

She shook her head.

He opened the door and ushered her forwards into the small cabin that consisted of a single room that had a bed in the right corner and a pair of comfortable looking armchairs nestled around a fireplace to the left.

Maya stepped inside.

Pyotr followed her.

The door shut behind him.

She turned to say that it was a charming place.

His hand closed around her throat.

Her back slammed against the wooden wall.

His growled words chilled her to the bone.

"You are mine now."

CHAPTER 13

Maya swallowed hard, her throat aching under Pyotr's fierce grip as he leaned towards her. She pressed back against the wall, her heart thundering and blood racing as fear sank icy claws into her heart and squeezed it.

"You are mine and I will not share you with anyone," he growled and pressed closer, gripped her throat harder.

She stared at him through wide eyes, reeling as his reaction to the male suddenly made a sickening sort of sense.

The females in his pride slept with more than one male, were shared between them all.

Her stomach turned, bile rising up her throat.

Pyotr moved closer still, pressing the length of his body against hers and pinning her to the wall with it. His grip on her throat loosened and he smoothed his palm over her cheek, the anger that had been in his golden eyes melting into a soft look, one that had her hackles rising and warning bells jangling in her head.

He canted his head and gazed at her, and she could almost fool herself into believing he was the male he had been outside, gentle and tender, caring.

But he wasn't.

He was far from those things.

Talon had been right about him.

Pyotr brushed his knuckles across her cheek, his gaze drifting to follow his hand, and he became absorbed in touching her, his air distant and lost.

She risked a glance at the door, the need to escape and find Grey pushing her to act.

His hand closed around her throat again and he growled low, a warning that rang through her and had her freezing against the wall, afraid he would go through with it and hurt her if she dared to move.

He rubbed his thumb along her jaw and over her chin, forcing her head up, so her eyes met his.

"I have been waiting so long for you," he murmured softly, warmth back in his eyes. A shadow shifted across them a moment later, chilling her. "My own female… my female to own."

Her stomach twisted again.

Gods, she needed to get away from him.

He lowered his hand to her chest and she tensed, going rigid as he slowly stroked his palm over her breasts, his eyes tracking his hand, darkness mounting in them as he touched her.

"I have been dreaming of this moment… of having you." He lifted his golden eyes to hers. "I have made a place for you in my cabin. I will keep you there, all for me."

She wanted to shake her head at that, the thought of becoming his captive sending her pulse rocketing faster, that fear squeezing her heart tighter. No. She didn't want to spend the rest of her life locked in a cage, a slave to this male, letting him do gods only knew what to her because he thought he owned her.

She wasn't an object.

The females of his pride might do whatever the males wanted, but she wasn't one of them, had been raised to be strong, to be something more than a whore, a breeding bitch for males.

She slapped his hand away.

Pyotr growled and shoved her back against the wall, using his strength to keep her pinned there, and she fought him as he dragged her skirt up and palmed her crotch.

"This is all for me," he snarled. "Get that into your head. You are mine now. Your brother gave you to me… and I will do as I please with you."

"No." She swung wildly with her left hand and he grunted as it connected, smacking hard into his cheek and knocking his head back.

She had been stupid to go along with this, for fooling herself into thinking it would work out fine and Talon had been wrong about Pyotr.

This wasn't where she wanted to be. She wanted to be with August, needed him with her and ached for him so fiercely, her heart crying out for him as she slapped at Pyotr, driving him away from her.

"Bitch." Pyotr caught her right fist when she tried to punch him and twisted her arm, ripping a cry from her lips as white-hot pain lanced her bones. He shoved her back against the wall. "Someone needs to teach you to respect the males of your species."

He pulled at her skirts and she kicked at him, frantically struggling to break free before he could do something terrible to her, something that would break her.

There was a knock at the door.

A familiar scent teased her senses, gave her comfort and strength.

Grey.

Pyotr glared at the door, collected himself and stepped back. He looked back at her as she righted herself and straightened her clothes with trembling fingers.

"You dare disobey me... and your family will pay."

Maya lifted her head to look at him.

He struck her hard across her cheek and she slammed into the wall near the door and collapsed to her knees, pain spider-webbing over her skull, her ears ringing, and the taste of blood blooming on her tongue.

The next thing she knew, gentle hands had her, gathered her into strong arms that tore down her strength and had her clinging to their owner as hot tears spilled down her cheeks. She buried her face in Grey's neck, unable to stop the sobs as they wracked her, and her heart and mind mocked her with the fact she had been stupid, an idiot to think coming here had been the right thing to do.

She had been a fool to believe that she would have a good life here, one where she was part of the pride, helped everyone who needed it and lived as part of their family, doing the duties of an alpha's mate.

She was going to end up shut in Pyotr's cabin, used whenever he wanted, treated as a slave. She would never see the light of day again.

Gods, it terrified her.

She squeezed her eyes shut, pressed closer to Grey and battled the fear rushing through her and the terrible things it whispered to her, evoking images that left her cold and trembling.

As the pain in her cheek faded, and those voices quietened, her strength slowly returned, Grey's gentle words of comfort and the shield of his arms around her restoring her balance and clearing her mind.

No.

Coming here had been her only choice. If she hadn't shown up, Pyotr would have dispatched his warriors to her pride, and she had the sickening feeling that they would have returned with Byron as their captive, so their alpha could make an example of her brother.

She had the feeling that if she disobeyed Pyotr now that he would do the same, only he would be making an example of Byron in front of her, showing her what happened when she didn't do as he wanted.

And if Byron's death wasn't enough to break her, Talon's or Grey's would follow.

Only she wasn't going to give him a chance to hurt her brothers.

"I'm going to kill him," she whispered against Grey's neck and he stilled.

"Not a good idea."

She didn't want to hear that. She pushed back, her senses stretching around her, beyond the walls of the cabin, monitoring everyone who moved around the village.

Two males stood outside the door, both of them from the group of three tigers that had come upon her and Grey in the forest.

A female was with them.

"I'm going to do it," Grey said, voice darker than she had ever heard it. He stood and she grabbed his wrist, stopping him. He looked down at her, his blue eyes glittering with frost. "I'm going to kill him for hurting you."

She shook her head and looked at the door. "There are too many of them."

Pyotr had an entire pride of warriors at his back.

If Grey tried to attack him, those warriors would be quick to defend their alpha, and she would lose her brother. Grey would become the first of her brothers that Pyotr killed in front of her, and she feared his death would be all it would take to break her. She couldn't lose him.

He turned stormy eyes on the door, his jaw tensing as his lips flattened in a hard line and his silvery eyebrows drew low.

She could feel his fury, his need to fight and punish the one who had struck her, and that it was hard for him to deny that need.

"Please, Grey," she whispered and he glanced at her, sighed as his shoulders sagged and he turned away from the door, coming to crouch in front of her. "He'll pay... but we need a plan... we need to do this together."

He opened his mouth to speak.

"I know you don't want me to fight," she said before he could utter the words, "but I need to fight. I need it..."

She held her hands out in front of her, drawing his focus to them, and to her nails. They were black, transformed by her hellcat genes and the need to fight she was battling to hold inside, to keep tamped down until she needed it. She wanted to go out there and launch herself into a battle just as he did, but it would only get them, and their pride, killed.

They needed a plan if they were going to succeed in taking Pyotr down.

Grey took hold of her hands and lifted his blue eyes to meet hers. "So what's this plan?"

She didn't have an answer to that question.

He smiled softly. "We'll think of something."

The door to her right opened, and the female she had sensed outside stood there, a petite blonde with dark gold eyes. She placed her hands in front of her pinafore and bowed her head.

"My alpha would like to announce his intention to hold the ceremony tomorrow night. He has posted two guards outside the cabin so you will feel safe while you prepare."

Maya wanted to laugh at that. Pyotr had placed the two males there to keep her from escaping, not to protect her.

Well, she wasn't going anywhere.

Not until Pyotr was dead and her pride, and her brothers, were safe from his wrath.

"If your brother would like to come with me."

Maya shook her head. "No. My brother will be staying with me until the ceremony to ensure that everything is done according to tradition."

The female quickly looked at her, surprise and fear flashing in her eyes, and then back down at her feet. Maya had the feeling that she expected Pyotr to punish her because Grey had refused to do as he wanted and was staying with Maya. What sort of male treated those he was responsible for in such a terrible way?

"As you wish. If there is anything you require, please speak with the guards." The female backed away from the door and closed it behind her.

Grey huffed beside Maya. "A satellite phone would be nice. Do you think he would agree to it?"

She frowned and looked at her brother. He scowled at his phone as he held it above him, moving it around, as if that was going to get him a signal.

"Why don't we just ask him to invite the pride to the ceremony?" Because that was as likely to happen as him giving them a phone so they could call for help.

Grey's lips tugged into a wry smile. "I could try leaving and going back down the trail until I get a signal."

Maya looked at the door. "I don't think that's going to happen. If you try leaving… I don't think you'll get far before he stops you."

And then she would be alone, without her brother to protect her.

"Quick thinking mentioning the tradition thing." He stood and shoved his phone into his jeans pocket, and held his hand out to her.

She took it and let him pull her onto her feet. They were unsteady, her legs trembling beneath her. He helped her to one of the armchairs and she sank into it, leaned her elbows on her knees and buried her fingers in her long hair, clawing it back as she held her head.

Grey dragged the second armchair close to hers and eased into it.

They had thirty-six hours.

Tradition stated that Pyotr couldn't see her in the thirty-six hours leading up to the ceremony, which was why he had chosen tomorrow night. He wanted it done as soon as possible.

The next she would see him would be at the ceremony.

She thought about it, going over everything she knew about traditional wedding ceremonies. Most tiger shifters didn't bother with them, but her parents and his had written it into the contract that bound them and he couldn't break from it, otherwise his claim on her could be broken and he wouldn't be able to retaliate against her or her pride.

So she had thirty-six hours to come up with a reasonable plan that wouldn't get her, Grey, and her kin killed.

She looked to her right, at Grey where he sat with his eyes locked on the door, a steely look in them. His anger flowed through her, together with a trace of despair, and a trickle of fear.

Gods, she was glad that he had insisted on staying with her until she was settled, because she might have been forced to go through with everything if he hadn't been around to help her.

He looked across at her, and gently placed his hand on her leg. "We'll get out of this mess."

She nodded. They would.

Together they were strong.

And she had just come up with a killer plan.

CHAPTER 14

August was going out of his fucking mind.

Talon had surprised him by answering his call to Underworld and saying that he would help him before August had even asked him, that whatever he planned to do, he wanted in on it, for Maya's sake.

He owed the tiger.

Talon had given him the Altay pride's location, and details of the nearest airport, and had agreed a time to meet him there.

Without Talon, August wouldn't have made it this far, stood in a small airport in a remote area of China, close to seeing Maya again.

Gods, he hoped they weren't too late.

Talon had painted a grim picture of the Altay pride's alpha.

The thought of his precious Maya being with that male made August's blood burn. He paced the tiny waiting room of the airport, his eyes constantly locked on the area passengers passed through after clearing customs. Every fibre of his being screamed at him to go ahead without Talon, to follow his instincts to Maya.

He tamped down that urge, aware that if he gave into it, it would take him days to reach her.

Talon knew the way to the Chinese border and had plotted the route they would take through the nature reserve to the Russian side.

To Maya.

Besides, he had the feeling Talon would kill him if he went off without him. The big tiger male wanted to be the one to save his little sister.

It wasn't going to happen.

August was going to save her, and he was going to kill the bastard who had her.

If they were lucky, they could reach the pride's village before Grey and Maya even made it there and cut them off. Grey's last message to Talon three days ago had mentioned continuing on foot from a location within China that was further away from the pride's village than the one Talon had picked as the border crossing.

Grey was doing his best to delay their arrival, his reluctance to hand Maya over to the Altay alpha showing in his actions, but the tiger thought he was only delaying the inevitable, giving Maya a little more time to enjoy her freedom.

He didn't know he had been buying August and Talon time too.

Time August was going to use to save her.

A fresh wave of people rolled through the doors and into the waiting area, and August stopped pacing, his eyes running over all of them, searching for one familiar face.

He needn't have searched so hard.

Talon stood head and shoulders above the other passengers, easy to spot as he sauntered out of the backroom with a pensive expression etched on his face, the black slashes of his eyebrows meeting hard above blazing amber eyes as he stared at his phone.

August's heart started a hard, painful beat.

He pushed through the people towards the tiger.

Talon lifted his head, and the flicker of fear in his eyes hit August hard.

"What?" He grabbed Talon's arm and pulled it towards him so he could see the screen.

There was a message on it, dated from yesterday, signed by Byron.

The ceremony was taking place today.

"Fuck," he growled and shoved Talon's hand away, the need to shift and run blasting through him as the desire to be with Maya now, before it was too late, exploded inside him. "Fuck!"

Talon clamped a hand down on his shoulder. "There's still time."

August unleashed a string of obscenities in response to that, because Talon didn't sound sure, and that sure as hell wasn't going to inspire him into believing that they could still reach Maya in time.

"Fuck it," he barked and stormed towards the exit. "Even if she's married the bastard... I'm going to kill him."

He shoved the glass door open and stepped out into the cool afternoon air, his gaze scanning the parked cars and the people coming and going.

His eyes caught on the mountains that rose in the distance.

Maya was there.

She needed him.

He dropped his pack, grabbed his thick red coat, and tugged it over his right shoulder.

Talon stopped him, seizing his wrist before he could remove it. "What the fuck do you think you're doing?"

"I'm going to her," August snapped and twisted his wrist free of the tiger's grip. "She needs me."

"By the time you get there, it'll be too late." Talon calmly stooped, picked up August's bag and slung it over his shoulder with his own pack. "Shift if you want… expose us all to humans… I'll probably see you at the border when I'm on my way back with Maya."

The black-haired male pivoted on his heel and walked away from him, swinging a set of car keys around the fingers of his left hand.

Bastard.

August tugged his coat back on and hurried after him, but it was hard to deny his urge to shift, and the pressing need to run. He caught up with Talon beside a silver compact car that looked far too small to fit both of them, and Maya and Grey, in it. Talon opened the driver's side door and squeezed into it, dumping their packs in the back seat.

It was tiny, but it was a vehicle, and hopefully once they were moving, the need to shift and run would abate.

He yanked the passenger door open and slid into the car as Talon started the engine. The male didn't hesitate, had pulled the car onto the road before August had even had a chance to put his seatbelt on and slammed his foot down on the gas, pushing the vehicle to its limit.

August gripped the handle on the door with one hand and the dashboard with the other as Talon wove through the cars on the road, veering in and out of the oncoming traffic at high speed.

Son of a bitch knew how to drive.

Or he was a maniac and was going to get them both killed.

Fear of ending up in a mangled mass of metal in a ditch had his need to shift and run shooting to the back of his mind as they sped towards Maya, his focus locked on just making it to the border in one piece.

He could worry about the rest once they got there and his feet were back on solid ground.

It wasn't long before they hit the end of the road and a dirt track. He grunted as the car bounced and dipped, rumbling over potholes and rocks. Ahead of them, the mountains loomed, swathed in green.

Maya.

He was coming.

"Fucking airport car-hire… place like this needs a good four-wheel drive," Talon muttered, his amber eyes locked on the road ahead as he manoeuvred the vehicle around a particularly deep pothole.

He could sense the tiger's frustration, his need to go faster, to reach Maya.

As soon as they hit the end of the track and the car rolled to a stop, August was out of the vehicle and stripping off his clothes, tossing them onto the seat. Talon followed him, his actions hasty and a little rough as he tore at his own clothing, ripping his t-shirt as he wrestled to get it off. The second he was naked, he dropped to all fours and shifted, growling as his body twisted and contorted, and fur rippled over his skin.

Looked like August was locking the car then.

He rounded the silver vehicle, pulled the keys out of the ignition and shut the driver's side door before locking it. He placed the key beneath the front tyre, and pushed the car, just enough that it rolled back onto the key and hid it.

The huge tiger beside him watched his every move, fascination in his bright gold eyes.

"You can tell me later how awesome I am for coming up with a great way of making sure we can get back into it." August dropped to his hands and knees.

Talon snorted, a low coughing sound that he figured was meant to be insulting and tell him that wasn't going to happen.

August closed his eyes and focused on the shift, gritting his teeth as his bones burned and fire swept over his skin. His body was quick to transform, years of practice making it take only a split second to shift from human into his snow leopard form, but it felt like longer, like every bone in his body was breaking as his legs shortened and altered, and his arms followed them, his fingers broadening as they shrank in length, and silver fur spotted with black rings sprouted from his skin and rippled up his arms.

He growled through his fangs as his face morphed, ears rising to the top of his head as his nose flattened and cheeks puffed up, and whiskers grew from them.

When his tail had finished forming, the part he liked least about shifting, he shook his head and let it ripple along his body, so his fur settled.

Talon took off.

August followed him into the woods, his heart and mind fixed on Maya, on the distance between them as it shrank.

He willed her to hold on, to feel that he was coming for her.

He had been a fool to let her go when he should have had the courage to fight for her, to break with tradition and win her over, to make her see that even if they hadn't been fated, he would have still been the one for her.

She was the only one for him.

It didn't matter what her pride wanted, or what his expected.

All that mattered was them being together.

Gods, he had been such an idiot to let her go.

He would never make that mistake again.

If the fates could just give him one more chance with her. Just one. He wouldn't fuck it up this time.

Once he had her back in his arms, he would never let her leave them.

He would hold on to her forever.

CHAPTER 15

Maya closed her eyes and took a deep breath. The air coming in through the small window of the cabin near the door smelled of evening. Her time was almost up.

She lifted her head when Grey touched her shoulder, his large hand warm and comforting, telling her that he could sense her feelings and he was there with her. For her.

Gods, she hoped this worked.

She looked down at herself, at the layers of gold fabric that criss-crossed over her breasts and swathed her body, cinched at her waist with a thick black satin sash. Her brother had helped her dress in the traditional outfit of a bride, his face like thunder the entire time, his blue eyes stormy and dark with a desire to fight, to draw blood for her sake.

It wouldn't come to the things he was imagining, she would make sure of that.

She wouldn't let Pyotr lay a finger on her.

Grey's blue eyes softened and he sighed, his bare chest shifting with it as he watched her, wrestling with his own feelings as fiercely as she fought hers. She had tried to get him to dress in a more traditional manner too, but he had forsaken his tunic in favour of the freedom to shift, and had stopped at donning a pair of loose black trousers tied around his waist with a black sash that matched hers.

Outside, someone jeered.

Her heart leaped about in her chest and she sucked down another breath, hoping to steady it. Pyotr wouldn't think anything was off if her heartbeat was fast, would think it was nerves, but she didn't want to give him any reason to focus on her too hard. Just the thought of him looking at her at all made her skin crawl and her head fill with the vile things he had said to her, and those he hadn't.

Those sick unspoken things he wanted to do with her.

She shuddered.

Grey gripped both of her shoulders. "You don't need to do this Maya. Stay in here and let me fight."

She shook her head, causing her black hair to brush across her exposed shoulders, and took his right hand, drew it away from her and kissed it.

Grey was strong, his hands callused and worn from all the battles he had fought, both in his tiger form and with a sword, but he wasn't strong enough to take on an entire tiger pride alone.

She would fight with him, at his side, once the deed was done and Pyotr was no more.

Without their alpha to lead them, half of the males would be drawn into fighting each other for the position at the head of the pride, and the rights it would grant them. It would be easy for her and her brother to pick off the weakest, and let the strongest kill each other while they fled.

A soft knock at the door had her heartbeat accelerating again.

Her time was up.

The nerves she had fought so hard to contain rose back to the fore, swift and fierce, a deluge that threatened to shake her courage. She steeled herself. She could do this. She was stronger than Pyotr and one part of the ceremony would give her the perfect opportunity to use that strength to end him.

Grey answered the door, revealing the same female who had come to them yesterday, only this time she wore a plain dark gold dress and she had bathed.

Pyotr wanted everyone looking just right for his special ceremony.

Maya curled her lip at that.

She turned on her heel, her bare feet making no sound on the wooden floor, and swept towards the door, meeting her brother there.

The female backed down the steps, her head bent the entire time, and kept backing away as her bare feet hit the dirt.

Maya followed her down the steps, aware of Grey as he prowled like a shadow behind her, a dark wraith waiting for his moment to strike. His need to fight flowed through her too, bolstered her courage and had her heart steadying as she reached the dirt and turned calmly towards her left, where the main cabin stood beyond the large fire burning in the centre of the village.

Eyes landed on her, intense and focused, more pairs than she had expected.

Her nerves jangled again but she held herself together and tamped them down. A few more to fight shouldn't prove a problem.

She lifted her chin and stared ahead of her. Blazing torches formed an aisle straight down the centre of the clearing, lined up between her and the fire. They circled the fire there, creating a path between them and the fire, and continued beyond it, lighting the way to the main cabin. Above her, the evening light had faded, and a million diamonds glittered against rich blue velvet.

It would have been beautiful, only the male standing at the end of the aisle in front of the fire wasn't the male she wanted.

She hesitated, the thought of walking towards that cruel bastard freezing her feet to the ground, doubts sparking to life inside her head and her heart, rousing a fierce need to run.

Grey placed his right arm under her left one and raised it, so her hand draped over the back of his.

That simple touch gave her the strength she needed.

If she stuck with the plan, it would all work out.

They had gone over it a thousand times, had thought of every possible thing. It would work.

She looked at the few females gathered near the first set of torches, only five in total. The other thirty or so attendees were all male, most of them wearing trousers tied with black sashes similar to Grey's. The males she could see near the front were another matter though. They were naked, ready to shift at a moment's notice.

That had her heart pounding again, that fear returning, worry that Grey was going to end up overwhelmed before he could even shift when she made her move.

Grey's fingers twitched beneath hers.

A silent message.

He would be fine.

He would. She would make sure of it. If everything went according to plan, it would be fine. She just had to hold her nerve until it was time.

She had thought that would be the easy part, but as Grey began walking her down the aisle, the instinct to run grew stronger, images flashing in her mind to taunt her with all the things Pyotr wanted to do with her, with how he wanted to break her.

It was a struggle to keep her eyes on Pyotr's as she approached him.

He watched her closely, the fire blazing at his back making him look like some unholy lord of Hell, casting highlights in his tousled sandy hair and glowing in his golden eyes. It shimmered over his bare shoulders, outlining his powerful body as he stood before her in only a small leather cloth marked with the sigil of his pride over his crotch.

Gods, she was thankful that tradition allowed her to be fully clothed.

She wasn't sure she would have had the courage to do this if she had been naked too.

The way Pyotr's golden eyes raked over her said she would be naked soon enough.

Alone with him.

She was counting on it.

Grey stepped aside when they reached Pyotr, passing her hand to him, and she didn't listen as Pyotr spoke the words. She said what was expected of her, somehow kept her eyes on his and her heartbeat level, as calm as she could manage.

When Pyotr turned away with her, she could feel Grey's desire to follow her and remain close to her. She glanced back at her brother, needing him to know that she was fine and to stick with the plan. She could do this.

She was stronger than Pyotr.

The bastard didn't know it though.

He was about to get one hell of a surprise.

They reached his cabin and he opened the door and extended the hand that held hers, encouraging her to step past him and into the wooden building. It was dark inside, made all the darker when Pyotr closed the door behind them.

Her eyes adjusted.

Widened.

She had been wrong. She had been the one to get one hell of a surprise.

She stared at the two females locked in cages at the opposite side of the room, near a double bed, both of them naked and dirty, huddled close to each other but separated by thick steel bars.

She whirled to face Pyotr.

"They were brides from other prides," he said casually as he lit a lamp, as if it was perfectly normal of him to keep females locked in cages. Her stomach churned, acid tossing like waves stirred by a violent storm, making her queasy, and an icy trickle spread through her veins. He lifted his head and looked at them, no feeling in his golden eyes, not a trace of guilt over what he had done, and then at her. "They were not promised to me. I found they had been with others. They were not only mine."

She tensed when he turned towards her, closed the gap between them with one stride, and raised his hand, sifting his fingers through her black hair.

"Unlike you," he murmured, voice distant as his golden eyes followed his fingers. "You have not been touched by another... have you?"

Maya quickly shook her head, but she couldn't stop herself from thinking about August, about that stolen moment in Underworld when he had changed her forever. Her heartbeat picked up, heat stirring in her veins to melt the ice.

Her eyes flicked towards the cages.

The fire inside her died, fear of ending up inside a cage rattling her courage and stealing her strength, making her legs tremble beneath her weight.

Gods, Pyotr was worse than the rumours, worse than she could have ever imagined.

She stared at the females as they watched her through dull, lifeless eyes.

Forced herself to look at what Pyotr had done to them, how he had broken them, abused them, just because they had dared to love another.

Her nerves settled.

Anger rose.

She would stop him.

She was going to end him.

She didn't fight him when he untied the black sash around her waist and began to undress her, continuing the tradition of their ceremony. She stood still and let him do it, her skin crawling as his eyes shone with excitement as he unravelled her robe, removing layer after layer.

Unwrapping her like a fucking present.

The gift that she was, from her pride to him.

Gods, she hated it.

It was degrading, painful, terrifying, but she had to weather it, had to allow it and wait for the right moment.

Her moment.

She was going to make Pyotr pay.

He stripped away the last layer, letting the material drift down her body to pool around her feet, the evidence of his arousal tenting his leather loincloth. It was hard to resist covering her nudity when he raked his eyes over her, looking at her as if he owned her, his gaze telling her all the sick things he wanted to do to her against her will.

"We skip the next part and skip straight to fucking you."

Maya shook her head and backed away a step, her heart lodging in her throat. "No. It's tradition and if you don't stick with it, this means nothing. I won't be yours."

He stopped undoing his loincloth and looked at her.

But then he continued, his eyes revealing nothing as he stripped it away and let it fall to the floor, revealing his hardness to her.

She refused to look at it, kept her eyes locked on his and her jaw set.

Silence stretched between them.

"Get on with it then." He jerked his chin towards her and stroked a hand down his shaft. "I will claim you the traditional way to satisfy the contract between our prides and then I will claim you my own damn way... with you on your knees as I take you from behind... and then you will be mine."

She would never be his.

Never.

Maya shifted, bones on fire as they shrank and grew, and snapped into new positions. She fell to all fours as amber fur striped with black swept over her skin and growled through clenched fangs as her head transformed and her tail sprouted from the base of her spine.

The second she was done, she adopted a submissive posture, lowering her body so her belly touched the wooden floor, and turned slightly to show the nape of her neck. Pyotr had to bite her there while in his tiger form, and then this part of the ceremony would be complete and they would shift back to continue with the mating.

She twisted a little further, luring him, her heart pounding erratically in her chest as she waited for him to take the bait.

Gold and black fur rippled over his shoulders and he snarled as he shifted.

The moment he hit the middle of his transformation, the point when he was at his most vulnerable, filled with pain and torn between two forms, she turned, pressed down hard with her back legs and reared up, raking her claws across his stomach and then kicking off.

She pounced on him, taking him down hard onto the wooden floor. He growled and completed the shift, far quicker than she had anticipated, and his back legs caught her in her stomach as he kicked, driving her off him.

Maya attacked again, leaped on his back and bit his shoulder, refusing to give up. She had started, and there was no backing down now. She had to finish this.

Pyotr twisted and bit her left leg, and she hissed and shoved with both of her paws, pushing him onto his side and away from her. She distanced herself and circled him, aware of the two females watching her as she kept her eyes locked on Pyotr's, unwilling to let him get the jump on her.

He bared his fangs and leaped.

Maya met him in the air, wrapped her front legs around his ribs and twisted with him, but he was heavier than her and she didn't stand a chance when he sank his claws into her shoulders and used that weight against her. She whimpered and hissed again as he slammed her onto the floor, his weight pressing down on her.

His head lunged towards her.

She quickly moved her head to block him, stopping him from reaching her nape.

Her teeth clashed hard with his and he growled as she snapped at him, hissing and driving him away. He backed off, his bright golden eyes studying her, looking for another opening.

She needed to keep his weight off her. She was stronger than him, but her strength meant nothing if he tilted her off balance. It would be too easy for him to best her.

His hind leg muscles twitched.

Maya leaped to her left as he sprung at her, and twisted, her back paws skidding on the ground and claws scraping over the wood as she propelled herself back towards him as he landed where she had been. She growled as she landed on his back, her claws cutting through his thick skin, leaving crimson trails in their wake, and grabbed the back of his neck in her teeth.

Pyotr roared.

Outside, all hell broke loose, the feral growls of his males filling the night air.

Grey.

Her momentary distraction was all Pyotr needed.

He easily shook her off him and before she could bring her focus back to the fight, he had her pinned beneath him on her back, his fangs gripping the front of her throat, cutting off her air.

No.

The edges of her vision grew hazy.

She struggled against him, kicking and scratching, hissing at him as he held her down and choked her.

Pyotr's grip on her throat tightened.

Pain swept through her like an inferno.

She tried to hold on to her tiger form, but the fire blazing through her burned it away.

Her neck shrank with her transformation back into her human form and she dropped free of his fangs, the back of her head striking the floorboards hard, sending more fiery agony sweeping through her.

She breathed hard, staring up at the tiger looming over her, her heart thundering as the sound of the battle raging outside stripped her strength away, fear for her brother and for herself overwhelming her.

If she gave up now, would Pyotr believe she had been merely trying to make their mating interesting for him, had simply wanted him to fight to claim her as his bride?

A familiar scent hit her.

Earthy.

Tinged with snow.

The urge to fight blazed back to life inside her, roused by her deepest instincts as they seized her.

Told her to fight for her territory.

To fight for her mate.

CHAPTER 16

August ran hard, his broad paws silent on the forest floor as he wove swiftly through the low hanging branches and scrub. It wasn't his natural terrain, but he had one hell of a leader to follow.

Talon raced ahead of him, a huge tiger bent on tracking the scent of his sister through the dark woods, not slowing even when the trees grew thicker, making it more difficult to weave between them at speed.

It pushed August to do the same, even as his muscles began to tire and the urge to rest grew inside him.

He couldn't rest.

Maya needed him.

All that stood between him and her was a punishing twenty mile run across mountains and through dense forest.

He would run three times that without stopping if it meant seeing her again.

Saving her.

He was almost there.

Gods, he hoped he wasn't too late.

Fuck it. Even if he was, he wasn't leaving without her and he knew Talon wasn't either.

They were taking her back.

And he would kill the bastard who had her to set her free.

His heart soared as golden light flickered through the trees in the distance ahead of him, and he caught the scent of other tigers in the area, markings left on the trees to ward off other shifters and declare the area as the territory of a pride.

Talon growled, letting him know that he had seen the fire too, and had smelled the tigers.

They were close.

Someone roared ahead of them.

Talon suddenly accelerated.

August struggled to keep up, fighting to remain on Talon's tail, refusing to let him reach Maya first, without him. He needed to be there, had to be the one to save her. A selfish desire but one he couldn't quite control as he pushed himself harder, lengthening his strides, and started to catch up with Talon and come up beside him.

The big tiger growled at him, golden eyes flashing with displeasure.

August growled right back at him.

Ahead of them, two more roars broke the night, together with the unmistakable sound of a fight.

What the hell was happening at the Altay pride?

Talon broke cover just ahead of him, and he followed a second later, didn't even hesitate as he hit the clearing and the small village of cabins nestled in it. He kicked off, sailing through the air over one large tiger to land on the back of another. The tiger growled as he sank his fangs into the nape of its neck and bit down hard, turning that growl into a pained whimper.

The big white tiger that had been thundering towards it snarled at him, giving him the same damned look Talon had back in the woods, one that reeked of irritation.

Grey.

Talon had warned him not to attack any white tiger with black stripes in the vicinity of the pride, because it was his brother.

It certainly made it easier for August to make sure he avoided attacking a friend in the fight.

Although Talon blended badly as he launched at two more tigers, hitting one in the side with his shoulder to knock him away and sending a paw slamming into the head of the second, driving his face down into the dirt.

Grey growled and pounced on the one Talon had knocked aside, savaging him with his claws and fangs.

August finished with his tiger and looked around at the fight, searching for Maya.

He couldn't see her.

He stood on the dead male and lifted his nose to the air, dragging it over his teeth to scent her.

Talon tossed his opponent aside, glanced his way and did the same, sniffing the air for his sister.

Grey growled and looked towards the largest cabin.

August roared and kicked off, launching himself towards it, heart hammering against his ribs as he caught her scent. Grey was right. She was in there.

With Pyotr.

The thought of that male touching her had him ripping through the first male foolish enough to attempt to stop him, using the agility that came with his smaller size to his advantage, moving too swiftly for the male to strike or bite.

He clamped his teeth down on the male's throat as he twisted the tiger beneath him and growled as he yanked his head upwards, ripping a hole in it. Blood sprayed over his paws and his chest, and the male shifted back to his human form, gasping as he struggled to hold on to the life slipping from him.

August didn't stop to watch him pass on to his ancestors.

He started running again, leaped over another tiger who tried to attack him and didn't look back when the male let out a pained snarl and the scent of blood in the air grew thicker. Talon and Grey were following him, tackling any foe that tried to stop him, giving him a clear run at saving their sister.

He wouldn't fail them.

He grunted as something slammed into his side, knocking the wind from him, and hit the dirt, rolling across it to land just right of the cabin.

He growled, shook his head as he tried to get his bearings, and pushed up onto his belly.

His senses sparked.

August sprang backwards, narrowly evading the male tiger that landed where he had been. The male growled and turned, kicked off and leaped towards him. August leaped left, dodging him again. The male's right paw slammed down onto his tail, claws raking along it to the tip as August moved it, pulling it free. Fire burned up the length of his tail and the scent of his own blood joined the others in the air around him. Damn. He tamped down the pain, locked it away and refused to let it overcome him.

The male rose up onto his back legs, standing far taller than August would if he did the same.

Snow leopards were smaller, but that just meant he had to be a little more cunning in a fight, and a little dirtier.

The male tiger came at him.

August shifted back into his human form and hurled himself towards the huge fire to his right. He twisted at the waist as his hip hit the dirt, blindly grabbed one of the logs and swung it upwards, towards the four hundred pounds of tiger about to land on him.

The tiger hissed and tried to evade, rotating his front half away from August in an effort to avoid the fire.

August didn't let him.

He shoved upwards, forwards, drove the damn torch into the bastard's fur and set it on fire.

The male took off, blazing a trail into the darkness.

August rolled onto his front and kicked off, the night air cold on his bare flesh, but the fire burning in his heart keeping him going, driving him onwards.

He leaped to the top of the cabin steps and shoved the door so hard it flew off its hinges and smashed into something metal.

As the light from the fire outside spilled into the cabin, his eyes widened.

A fucking cage?

Was this bastard serious?

Someone growled at him.

August casually swung his gaze towards the owner of it.

The big male tiger hunkered down, his fur already dotted with blood. It coated his mouth too.

August saw red.

He growled and shifted in a heartbeat, met the male as he launched towards him, grappling with him. The moment his back paws hit the floor again, he shoved upwards as hard as he could, driving into the male with all of his strength, tipping him off balance.

The male hit the wall.

August's gaze zeroed in on his exposed neck.

He snarled and launched forwards, towards it, his jaws parting as he angled his head and aimed for the male's vulnerable spot.

A huge paw struck him hard in the side of his head, sending him into the wall on his right, and then came again, claws raking over his fur and drawing blood, sending more fire sweeping through him.

A feral roar echoed around the cabin, deafening in volume.

Maya slammed into the male, her bare pink skin marred with blood around her throat and on her hips and thighs. She growled through her short fangs and hooked her arm around the tiger's throat, dragging him backwards.

Exposing the male's vulnerable spot again.

August launched at it.

The male broke free of Maya's grip and barrelled into him, sending him skidding backwards. The bastard didn't stop. He ploughed onwards, until August hit the wall near the door. He tried to escape, but the male didn't give him the chance. Sharp fangs sank into his right shoulder and he cried out as pain tore through him, and struggled to hold on to his snow leopard form.

Maya snarled and suddenly the male tiger was gone, ripped away from him and sent flying across the cabin. He struck the far wall and hit the floor, shook his head and growled as he came to face them again.

She stepped in front of August, shielding him with her bare body, facing the male.

Beautiful.

She had every instinct inside him awakening, rising to overwhelm him, from a desire to claim her to a desire to defend her, and all the ones in between.

Before he could even move a muscle, she had kicked off, was on the tiger and fighting him, a wild warrior who stole his breath as she grappled with the tiger, hands clutching his front paws, head ducking and dodging as the male tried to bite her.

She growled and twisted, and threw the male to her left, towards the cages.

Gods.

She glanced at him, that blue corona in her glowing golden eyes again.

Talon had told him her secret. Their secret. August had been right.

She had hellcat blood in her.

On a low snarl, she launched at the male, catching him before he could gather himself, landing on his back and gripping his jaw with one hand and his neck with the other. The tiger snarled and bucked, trying to shake her, but she held on to him, her eyes flashing dangerously as she fought against him, wrestling with his head.

August had foolishly thought he would be the one to fight the alpha for her, that she would need him to come charging in like a white knight to save her. Idiot. Maya was strong. Beautiful. She didn't need him to fight her battles for her.

She needed him to fight her battles *with* her.

At her side, as an equal.

She yanked on the tiger's head as he snarled, grunted and cried out as she fought him, her fingers bleeding as she clutched his upper jaw and pulled, his teeth sinking into her delicate flesh.

She roared as she leaned back and managed to pull the tiger's head up at last.

Giving August the opening he needed.

This time, he wouldn't waste it.

They would end this male together.

August ran at the male and roared as he closed the distance between them. The male frantically fought Maya but she held him firm, her eyes almost entirely blue now as they shone with the desire that echoed in August, a deep need to make the male pay.

Gladly.

August growled and seized the male's throat, bit down hard and locked his jaw, so the male couldn't break free. The metallic tang of blood filled his mouth and the male struggled, but August held on, biting down harder as Maya fought to keep the male's head up. The taste of her blood joined the male's in his mouth and fury blasted through him, driving all the light from him, rousing a dark need to avenge his mate.

He snarled and shook his head, ripping through the male's neck, spilling his blood.

The male's struggles slowed, the scent of his blood growing stronger in the air, the warmth of it rolling down August's throat to his stomach and over his chest.

When the male sagged, collapsing beneath Maya, August released him and staggered back a step, shifting as he did so and landing on his bare backside, breathing hard.

Maya threw her head back and roared.

Silence fell like a shroud over the village.

August lifted his eyes and looked at Maya where she straddled the dead tiger, her eyes glowing blue and gold, her chest heaving as she fought for air.

Gods, his fated one was beautiful.

A warrior.

She growled low in her throat, eased onto her feet and prowled towards him, a fire in her eyes that said she wanted him, here and now, wanted to stake a claim on him.

Fuck, he wanted to claim her too.

Just not right now.

He held his right hand up to her, turned his face away and vomited.

"August!" Maya was by his side in an instant, the hunger that had been burning in her eyes replaced with concern as she took hold of his shoulders and made him look at her.

He shook his head, swallowed and tried to keep it down, and failed dismally. He quickly turned away and threw up again, just the sight of the tiger beyond her and the blood pooling beneath it enough to have his stomach rebelling.

He stared down at the blood he had vomited up, and threw up again. Fantastic. Not exactly how he had pictured this moment going. Maya should have been throwing herself into his arms right about now.

She rubbed his back instead, making him feel a million times worse.

"That's a lot of blood," she said.

So he threw up again.

Hung his head and prayed to his ancestors that the floor would open up and swallow him whole.

Or maybe he could die from shame.

Maya reached for him, but then sharply withdrew her hand. He lifted his head to ask why she didn't want to touch him, fearing her answer, and his words died on his lips when he found her gazing at her upturned palms.

Blood covered them, seeping from the shallow cuts caused by the tiger's teeth.

August shot to his feet, snatched a towel from the small bathing area near the right wall of the cabin, and was back to her before she could even turn her head to track his movements. He sank to his knees in front of her, ripped the dark towel in half, and gently bound her left hand and then her right, tying the cloth tight enough that it would stem the bleeding.

He lifted his eyes, but they didn't make it to hers. They caught on her throat.

He growled and reached for her, pure fury blasting through him as he took in the deep puncture wounds on the side of her neck, where the bastard had clearly gripped her with his fangs.

Before he could touch them, she was in his arms, her face buried in his neck and her arms around him.

He stared at his outstretched hand, absorbing the feel of her against him. She was warm. Trembling. He closed his eyes, wrapped his arms around her and held her gently, keeping her tucked close to him.

Where she belonged.

The feel of eyes on him roused a desire to growl at their owners, but he tamped it down, not wanting to frighten the females as they looked between him and the dead tiger. Tears lined their lashes and tumbled down their dirty cheeks, their relief written in every line of their faces.

Another pair of eyes landed on him.

He looked up at their owner, nodded when Talon stared at Maya, concern edged with fear in his stormy amber eyes. The male nodded, and glared at the cages, and then at the dead tiger.

Talon didn't say a word. He quietly went to work breaking the locks on the cages and freeing the females, covering them with thin blankets and ushering them outside with Grey's help.

Maya remained hidden in August's arms, her warm breath skating over his neck, her bandaged hands resting softly against his back, her arms looped beneath his.

Gods, it felt good to hold her again, to feel her in his arms and know he never had to let her go.

He would never let her out of his sight again.

He smoothed his right hand over her hair and savoured the feel of it, as new to this as she was, unsure what he was meant to do or say. He had never felt this close to anyone, especially a female. He had spent his life keeping relationships short and sweet, all business. He wasn't sure he had ever cuddled anyone.

It felt fucking wonderful.

He lowered his head and pressed a kiss to the top of her head, breathed her in and closed his eyes.

She drew back, stealing the moment from him, and raised her head, her amber eyes round as she looked at him.

There was relief in them, and hope. A lot of hope.

Something else too, something that stole his breath and stirred a need to kiss her to show her that she wasn't alone, she wasn't the only one feeling new things, things that caught him off balance.

Although he couldn't fall any further than he already had for her.

Her soft gaze dropped to his mouth, and her dark eyebrows pinched in a frown.

He went to wipe his hand across his mouth to clear the blood away, but she beat him to it, rubbing it away with the bandage around her right hand.

And then her mouth was on his.

Stealing his heart all over again.

He gathered her closer, pulled her onto his thighs and kissed her, lost himself in her and the relief that washed through him, carrying away his fears and his strength with it. Gods, he had feared. He had feared he would be too late. He had feared he would lose her. He had feared she wouldn't want him and that he had been wrong about them.

All of those fears melted away as she kissed him deeply, desperately, as if she couldn't get enough of him either.

He slipped his arm beneath her knees, wrapped his other one around her back, and scooped her up as he stood, his lips still on hers, their kiss not slowing.

He was going to kiss her every damn step of the way back to the car.

Every step of the way home.

He was never going to stop kissing her.

He was never going to stop craving her.

When she was ready, he would become her mate, her only male.

Until then, he wasn't letting her out of his sight.

He wasn't going to let her go again.

CHAPTER 17

August's plan to keep her with him had hit a snag just a single step outside the cabin in the Altay pride's village.

Maya secretly smiled to herself behind the thick red scarf covering the lower half of her face in the way she always did whenever she relived that moment. She had been so caught up in him, in how good it had felt to be back in his arms, that it had taken her a moment to realise why he had stopped.

Talon and Grey had blocked his path down the steps, both of them far too naked for her liking, their powerful arms folded across their bare chests and their bright eyes locked on her.

August had done his best to cover her so her brothers and the subdued members of the Altay pride didn't see anything, and had told Talon and Grey that they were leaving, and he was going to take her to his home.

Her heart had done a strange flip in her chest at that.

While part of her had wanted to rebel, everything she had been through pushing her to escape his hold, afraid he would be like Pyotr, her heart had calmed her and told her that everything would be perfect if she went with him, that he would never force a bond upon her or treat her as Pyotr had treated his females.

He would be gentle, tender, and would take care of her.

His eyes had told her more than that when he had looked at her, promising her that he would never try to overpower her or control her, that he wanted her to stand at his side as an equal, as his partner.

Talon had sort of obliterated the moment when he had told August no.

Grey hadn't helped when he had denied her fated one too, stating that she needed to go back to their pride.

August had looked at her then, and gods, she had wanted to tell him to ignore them and run away with her.

But her brothers had been right.

She still hated the way August had looked at her when she had told him that, and announced she would return to her pride.

He had looked as if she had plunged a knife into his chest and twisted it.

So she had been quick to give him a balm to soothe his pain, telling him that it would be a temporary parting, a necessary one because she and her brothers needed to speak with Byron about everything that had happened.

August's silvery eyes had softened then, and although she had sensed his reluctance to let her go and his fierce need to keep her with him, he had agreed to it.

On the basis that she come to him within two weeks.

Her smile widened.

Gods, she had loved the way he had growled that he would go 'fucking insane' if she kept him waiting any longer than that.

Byron looked back at her, knocking her out of her memories.

She shivered as a frigid wind swept down the broad valley in front of her, whipping up ice flakes and blasting them into her yellow waterproof jacket and black trousers.

Byron's gold eyes told her everything he was feeling, and she agreed with him about a few things. Most notably how it was too damn cold up on the mountain and that August was already insane because he lived in this unholy place.

The snow crunched beneath her boots as she trudged onwards, trailing close behind Byron as he followed their guide along the narrow path at the base of a towering cragged mountain.

Maya looked off to her right, her breath catching as she glimpsed the village nestled on the plateau high above her for the first time.

August was there, waiting for her and her brother.

Could he feel she was close now?

Did he want to run to her as she wanted to run to him?

It had only been nine days, but she had missed him, had been going out of her mind, needing to be close to him again.

It turned out she was the one who had gone fucking insane.

Byron had grown so sick of her switching between moping around the village and arguing with him that he had stepped up her departure, bringing her to Bhutan four days early.

Her brother had wanted to make August wait right until the fourteenth day before bringing her to him.

She could understand her brother's reluctance. He had been genuinely distraught when Talon and Grey had told him everything she had been through, and had apologised to her countless times since then.

He had also smothered her, refusing to let her out of his sight.

It had taken threatening to leave and go to August with Talon and Grey's help to make him confess that he didn't want her to go, that he was worried August might hurt her, that she might not be happy with him.

Maya had told him to come with her and meet August for himself.

She wanted her brother to see that August was the only one in the world who could make her truly happy.

"Is it not quicker that way?" Byron hollered over the wind and pointed towards the sweeping valley to their right that separated them from the village.

The guide, a male dressed in neon green protective clothing, laughed. "Only if you're talking about meeting your death."

She frowned at the back of the male's head.

He looked over his shoulder at Byron and swept his right hand out. "This whole area is riddled with crevasses. Only a mad person would choose that way."

Maya was considering it.

The trail was taking too long.

She could feel August was close now and she needed to see him again, would risk death to achieve that.

Byron pushed the hood of his black jacket back to reveal the dark orange woollen hat he wore over his black hair and looked back at her, his amber eyes warning her that he had sensed her need to run. He glared at the white world around them.

"It's fucking horrible here," he muttered from behind the black scarf wrapped around his nose and the lower half of his face.

Maya looked around her.

It was beautiful.

The journey had been long, and a little frightening in places.

They had landed at the local airport yesterday and had been met by their guide, who had driven like a demon along a track that had taken them deep into the forest. From there, it had been a long walk along trails that had followed the course of a river, bringing them past splendid waterfalls as they rose higher into the hills.

After camping in the forest, they had trekked across open land and arrived at the base of a sheer cliff several hundred feet tall.

Their guide had climbed it as if it was nothing, no rope to protect him if he fell.

When he had reached the top, he had dropped a rope and harness for them. Byron had insisted on going first, not trusting the strength of the rope. She had the feeling he was going to be overly protective of her for a while, his guilt driving him to coddle her.

Talon and Grey had given him hell when they had return to the pride with her.

For the sake of Byron, they had waited until they were alone, none of the pride within earshot, but they had really given him both barrels.

She had to admit that she had given him a little hell of her own too, had made it very clear that his behaviour over the past few decades had hurt her, and that she wasn't something he could trade like a commodity.

She was his sister.

His flesh and blood.

Byron had been quiet for a few days after that, withdrawn from the world, more distant than he had ever been. Whenever she had started to feel guilty, Grey had reminded her that Byron had brought it upon himself, and that he deserved to suffer for what he had done. He did, she felt that too, but he was also her brother, and despite the things he had done, she still loved him and it hurt her whenever she saw him in pain.

When he had finally talked to her, it had been to apologise, to beg her forgiveness and to ask her to put him out of his misery, because he wanted to make everything right.

She only had to tell him what to do.

Maya had told him straight that there was only one thing he could do.

Let her be with August.

She could understand his wariness, but his fear was misplaced.

August would never hurt her.

She was going to make her brother see that.

She stared up at the plateau.

Gods, she needed to see August.

The trail swept around a bend and her breath left her in a rush as the beauty of the world August called his home hit her full force.

The trek had been hell, but gods, it had been worth it.

She was starting to see how August managed to live up here, high on the mountain. Such a view was worth putting up with a little cold.

It felt as if she could see the whole world.

The valley dropped below her, a swath of white that ended at the cliff. Beyond it, the green of the forest stretched far, covering the lower half of the mountain range. At the bottom of the winding valley, a river glittered in the sunshine, and the spray from a waterfall caught the light, casting a rainbow. On the other side of the river, mountains rose again, coated with green at their bases but fading to pure white at their cragged peaks.

The valley extended forever, forking into more valleys to her left, and dropping into the plain to her right.

Above them, the sky was purest blue, the sun bright and dazzling.

"Maya," Byron said, and she realised she had stopped walking.

She looked over her left shoulder at him and smiled, unable to contain it. His amber eyes narrowed with the smile his scarf hid, and he held his gloved hand out to her.

She went to him but didn't take his hand. He turned away from her and kept walking, catching up with their guide. She looked up ahead of her at the plateau.

As she drew closer to it, awareness of August grew inside her, becoming stronger with every step she took.

He was waiting for her.

She wanted to be there now, in his arms again, but the damned trail turned away from the village and continued to skirt the edge of the mountain.

Maya fought for patience. She had been waiting days to see him again. A few more minutes wouldn't kill her.

She felt eyes on her.

Lifted her head.

Her heart soared.

Ahead of her on the path, a lean figure clad in a red jacket and black trousers was striding towards them, his footing sure on the slippery trail.

August.

His wild hair matched the colour of his jacket, tousled by the wind as he hurried towards her, his handsome face shifting from a pensive look to one of sheer relief edged with a note of desperation as he spotted her. His pace quickened, until he was jogging.

His silver eyes were dazzling in the sunlight, liquid precious metal with a corona of gold in their centres around his dilated pupils.

She was sure her own amber eyes were equally as bright, a blue shimmer around her pupils that gave away her excitement and her heritage.

She was past Byron and their guide in a heartbeat, running to meet August.

He swept her up into his arms the moment she was within reach and spun with her, holding her high above him. She planted her hands on his strong shoulders and smiled down at him. He slowly lowered her, his smile fading as his gaze dropped to her lips, and her heart kicked in her chest, anticipation fluttering in her belly.

She let her hands slip from his shoulders and tangled one in his short red hair, ripping a low growl of pleasure from him.

"Gods, I missed you," he rasped so earnestly that her heart warmed and melted a little.

Before she could tell him that she had missed him too, his lips were on hers, searing her with their heat, chasing away the cold that had seeped into her bones despite the thick layers of clothing she wore.

His grip on her tightened, his left arm banding around her waist, hand clutching her ribs, and his right hand holding her backside.

She lost herself in his kiss, in his taste, her heart singing and soaring.

Someone cleared their throat.

They broke apart.

Surprisingly, it wasn't her brother.

The guide rolled his pale golden eyes. "You were meant to stay at the village."

August glared at him. "I am at the village."

The male huffed, pulled his scarf down and shoved the hood of his green jacket back, revealing long silver-gold hair tied in a ponytail.

"This is not the village." The male pointed towards the plateau. "*That* is the village."

"It's the path to the village," August countered, and Maya had the feeling their guide was more than just a regular member of the pride.

He ran his hand over his hair in a way that screamed of frustration. "I said I would make sure she reached you safely... to trust me with her... and you said you would."

"I did... I do... but she's here now." August grinned up at her. "Come on, Dalton... don't ruin the moment. Be mad at me later."

Dalton huffed again. "I'll be mad at you now. What were you thinking running down the path like that anyway? One slip and you end up down there."

When Dalton pointed, Maya looked down, and her stomach turned at the drop to the valley and the wide crevasses that ran across it like scars, dark blue in their depths.

"I have good footing," August said, and she realised he was talking to her when he gently lowered her to the trail. "I wouldn't have dropped you. Dalton is just trying to frighten you."

She got the impression Dalton was trying to scare some sense into August, not frighten her.

Byron growled. August narrowed his eyes on her brother.

Gods, she wasn't sure she was ready for this.

Talon had called to tell her that he had spoken with August and clued him into the fact he needed to win Byron's approval or her brother was unlikely to leave without her. She just hoped that August could hold back the anger she knew he felt on her behalf.

He blamed Byron for what had happened to her.

She blamed her brother too, but she knew when to forgive and forget, and this was one of those times. She wanted to be with August, without the constant threat of interference from Byron, free to live her life how she wanted, and to achieve that she was willing to let go of the past and focus on her future.

August needed to do the same if he wanted to be with her.

She turned her back to August, coming to face Byron. "So... this is August. August, this is my brother, Byron."

August extended his hand over her right shoulder. Byron looked as if he wasn't going to take it and then reached past Dalton to shake it.

She squeaked when August wrapped his arm around her waist and squeezed her, bringing her back into contact with his front. Gods, he was so warm. She wanted to snuggle into him and hibernate.

Among other things.

"Come... let's get you both warmed up." He took her hand and led the way along the trail.

Dalton muttered things behind her about how a pride's alpha was meant to be safe at all times, and how reckless August could be.

He didn't sound angry though.

He sounded as if he had expected August to meet them here, had known his alpha wouldn't be able to wait for them to reach the village, and was thankful August had been able to hold on this long before coming to her.

She was glad that he had too.

She didn't like the thought of him climbing down the cliff face.

Being hauled up it had been frightening enough.

"It was nice of you to agree to come here to meet me," August said over his shoulder, and glanced back at her brother. There was a shimmer to his silver eyes that made him look mischievous. As he turned away, he spoke in a low voice. "The cold might slow you down enough to stop you thinking about trying to kill me."

She smiled at that.

She could feel the trickle of dread that ran through his feelings as he clutched her hand and led the way towards the village. She squeezed his hand, silently letting him know that she wouldn't let Byron kill him.

He was wrong about her brother anyway.

Byron had been upset by what had happened, but he had taken making reparations with the Altay pride and the ruling council of their kind in his stride, had been willing to do whatever it took to smooth things over.

Thankfully, the council had been on her brother's side when they had heard her account of what had happened and the accounts of the females Talon and Grey had freed from Pyotr's cages.

Her pride's reputation had remained intact, and the Altay pride had been handed over to another pride in the area, one who would make sure the surviving males were reformed and the females were taken care of in the future, given the rights they deserved.

Byron hadn't come all this way to kill August.

He had come here to thank him.

Although she did suspect that there might be some growling involved and a few death stares, and the odd threat about what would happen to August if he didn't take care of her.

She stared up at the back of August's head, letting the fact she was finally with him again soak in.

It felt as if the journey here had been long, difficult, and it had challenged her, pushed her to her limits, but it had been worth it.

She had been tested, they both had, but now they were finally together.

Nothing would keep them apart.

His head turned slightly and he looked at her out of the corner of his eye, his lips curved into a soft smile, as if he knew her thoughts and he liked them.

"Not far now," he said as they left the trail and hit a wide expanse of snow.

Footsteps littered it, and there were places where it had been tamped down, marked with long scrapes.

Someone had been playing there recently, making snowballs.

One whizzed past her head.

She barely dodged it.

August growled, stopping dead and pivoting on his heel to face whoever had thrown it.

A young girl in a pink jacket and purple trousers stood frozen a few metres away, wide silver eyes full of fear. The boy she had been playing with crouched closer to Maya, his back to August, little shoulders rigid beneath his jacket.

Maya released August's hand and stooped, and felt his eyes on her as he turned her way. She gathered a handful of snow, formed it into a small loose ball, and tossed it gently towards the little girl.

It tapped her on the leg and broke apart, showering snow onto her black boots.

The girl looked down, frowned and then looked up at her. "You make bad snowballs."

Maya smiled, hoping to hide that it had been the point. She was hardly going to make a solid snowball and hit a child with it.

August maybe, but not a child.

"You'll have to show me how it's done," she said, and the girl beamed at her, her fear forgotten. "We'll make a play date… if you'd like that?"

The girl nodded.

The boy shot to his feet so fast he slipped, and August had to snatch his wrist to keep him from falling on his backside.

"Me too," the boy said as he stood with his arm hanging from August's hand, holding him upright.

She nodded. "Of course."

The boy and the girl glanced at August.

He released the boy.

"If… it's okay… with…" the boy stammered, his pale gold eyes locked on August.

Maya stooped while August was distracted, scooped up a handful of snow and rose back on her feet.

August cocked a red eyebrow at the boy. "She's free to do as she pleases."

That was good to hear.

Because right now she wanted to do this.

She tiptoed, caught the hood of his red jacket and shoved the snow down his back.

August roared and twisted, tugging at his jacket as he spun in a circle, a pained look on his face.

The boy and girl laughed hard, and she giggled along with them as he fought to get the snow out.

A few of the people passing by stopped to stare, some of their lips twitching as they struggled not to laugh at their alpha too. Two of the females cast her smiles that warmed her, eased her nerves and made her feel welcome.

"Godsdammit." August shuddered and pulled at the bottom of his jacket, and snow tumbled out of it.

He stilled, his eyes locking on her.

A shiver ran down her spine.

Her instincts screamed to run.

"*You*," he said in a low voice.

Maya shrieked and ran.

She made it two steps before August had tackled her, taking her down into the snow. She fought him, laughing the whole time as he struggled to pin her down. He grinned when he finally caught her shoulder, and she shook her head, her eyes wide as he gathered a handful of snow.

"You wouldn't."

His smile said that he would.

"I'm a guest—"

Her words cut off in another shriek as he quickly tugged on the front of her jacket and stuffed the snow down it.

It was a smaller amount than she had thrown down his, and he had only shoved it between her jacket and jumper, but it was freezing, sending a blast of cold over her chest.

She shivered, teeth chattering as she pushed him off her and rolled to her knees, and opened her coat.

The snow dropped out, leaving her dark orange jumper covered in white flakes.

"Oh, this is war," she said.

August was on his feet before she could grab him, his kissable lips curved in a broad grin that made her heart thump harder.

Gods, he was gorgeous.

Hers.

Dalton cleared his throat.

August froze and looked at him.

Maya beaned him in the side of his head with a snowball.

It rolled off his face, down his chest, and hit the snow with a thump.

He sighed and shook his head. "I'll get you back for that later."

He held his hand out to her.

Maya placed hers into it.

And pulled him down into the snow with her.

He landed on top of her and stared down into her eyes, his silver ones bright with excitement, with happiness.

He dropped his head to kiss her.

Dalton cleared his throat again, a little harder this time. Byron huffed.

August groaned, rolled off her and helped her onto her feet, muttering under his breath, "Spoilsports."

She was right there with him, but she supposed Byron had come all this way to meet with him as two alphas, and August was so swept up in her that he was probably making a bad impression.

Although, the warmth in Byron's amber eyes said that wasn't the case at all.

He looked happy.

For her.

"I didn't climb up a mountain to watch you two frolicking in the snow," Byron growled with no trace of real anger in his tone and followed Dalton as the male led him deeper into the village.

He liked seeing it though. He liked seeing her happy.

"Is your brother always this gloomy?" August said as they trailed behind them.

Maya thought about that as she glanced around the village, meeting the eyes of some of the pride and smiling at them. "Always. He used to smile… before our parents died and he became alpha."

August nodded. "He sounds like Cavanaugh. He was alpha before me, but he didn't want it. He wanted the freedom to choose his mate, to be with his fated one, but tradition expected him to mate with a highborn female."

She stilled, heart thumping hard against her chest and all the warmth rushing out of her.

August stopped and looked back at her. He shook his head, stepped towards her and caught her cheek, tipping her head up so her eyes met his.

"Fuck tradition." He lowered his head and kissed her, sweeping away her fears, the thought that he might not want her as his mate after all and might choose one from among his pride, forcing her to see him with another. He broke away from her lips, pressed his forehead against hers, and sighed. "You're the only one I want, Maya. If it meant giving up the pride as Cavanaugh did, I would do that so I could be with you."

She pressed her brow harder against his and nuzzled him, his words warming her heart and chasing the chill from it.

She felt the same way.

If she had to give up everything, she would do it without hesitation.

She would do anything to be with August.

Not because he was her fated one.

Because she was in love with him.

CHAPTER 18

It was hard to keep from looking at Maya as she sat on his couch. He had meant it when he had told her that he had missed her. He had lost his fucking mind just one day after they had parted, before he had even made it home, and had gradually been going more and more crazy ever since.

It had really pushed Dalton to his limit.

August had shoved him right past it when he had received word that Byron and Maya were coming to visit.

It had taken a two-hour-long argument for Dalton to convince him that his place was at the pride, waiting there to meet Byron and greet them, as an alpha should.

August had only caved when Dalton had promised he would be the one to pick them up at the airport, and he would get them to the village as quickly as possible without compromising their safety.

Still, it had taken over a day.

Gods, he hadn't slept a wink last night.

He had lain awake thinking of Maya, wondering where Dalton had set up camp and whether she was afraid to be in a strange forest.

One where tigers roamed.

He glanced at her again, fielding a frown from her brother.

There was so much he wanted to talk to her about. He wanted to know everything that had happened while they had been apart. He wanted to know everything about her life up until this point. He wanted to know all of her.

But most importantly, he needed to ask her a question.

One that had him fighting a bout of nerves that threatened to have his leg jiggling as he sat in the armchair, trying to make polite conversation with Byron, when all he wanted to do was be alone with her.

Okay, maybe he wanted to punch Byron first, and then be alone with her.

The bastard deserved it.

He didn't care how apologetic the male had been after discovering what had happened to Maya and what sort of sick twisted son of a bitch he had given his sister to. Byron deserved to suffer. He deserved to go through the same hell as Maya had.

She glanced at him, a trickle of fear running through the feelings he could sense in her.

He reined in his anger, aware that she could feel it in him.

If being genial to Byron would get him out of his life and hers, then he would suck it up and not slug the bastard.

Gods, he just wanted to be alone with Maya.

The pride had taken his abolition of the tradition regarding mating well, only a few members grumbling about it. All of them from highborn families. Most of the pride had been pleased, happy for him when he had told them he had found his fated one, and that he hoped she would be coming to stay with him, and with them.

His heart had swollen with pride as he had walked her through the village. So many of his kin had come to meet her, offering her warm greetings and smiles, showing their eagerness for her to join the pride.

He hadn't imagined it going so well.

He hadn't been prepared for them to welcome Maya like that.

Gods, he was fortunate to be the alpha of such a wonderful pride, one that had survived adversity and come out of it stronger than ever, not only physically, but emotionally. It had strengthened their love, their desire to cherish everything they held dear, and their need to protect one another.

It had given them the strength to stand with him, to speak up and renounce the outdated traditions of their kind, freeing themselves from their bonds and allowing them to be with whoever they desired, to embrace love wherever they found it. Life was too short to live it any other way.

He had leaped that hurdle and now there was only one that stood between him and Maya.

One little question.

Byron curled his lip at August's home, looking over everything with an air of disdain.

August curled his fingers into fists, and savoured the fantasy of slamming one into the male's face.

Dalton scowling at him had him straightening his fingers and resting his hands over his knees instead. His friend didn't have to worry. He wasn't going to hit the male. As much as he hated him for what he had done, he was Maya's brother, and his beautiful female was kind, caring and gentle enough that she still loved her brother even after everything he had put her through. So punching Byron's lights out was a no go, and only because he didn't want to upset her.

Byron's amber eyes darkened. "You live in a rather inaccessible place."

August shrugged. "It works for us. We rarely have any trouble from outsiders up here."

Just the once, when Archangel had come and slaughtered half the village. It was something they had in common. Both of their prides wanted the hunter organisation to pay for what it had done.

"I did have you winched up rather than making you climb the cliff," he said.

Byron glared at him again. "I could have scaled it."

August doubted that, but didn't call the male on it.

He sipped the drink Dalton had made, enjoying the burn as it went down. Maya toyed with her own mug, turning it back and forth in her hands. Hands he wanted to feel on him.

Her amber gaze slid to him, her pupils dilating as their eyes met.

Fuck, it was hard to concentrate when she was throwing off signals he could read loud and clear, could feel in her. She wanted him. She wanted to be alone with him as fiercely as he did, wanted to pick up where they had left off in that booth back in Underworld.

His left leg jiggled. He put his hand on it and shoved down, stopping it from moving.

"Where's Grey? I figured he would come with you," he said and she lifted her head higher and pinned him with bright gold eyes that only increased the need to sweep her up in his arms and take her somewhere private.

"Our brother is away," Byron said for her. "On business."

Something about the way Byron said that with a sharp bite in his tone, and the worried look Maya cast at her brother, warned August that he was lying, and neither of them knew where Grey was.

Maybe he was taking a break from the pride.

Talon had told him about Grey, about how their parents had assigned him to protect Maya and Byron rarely allowed him to leave the pride because she was always there.

August couldn't blame the male if he had decided to take an extended vacation from the pride to enjoy his newfound freedom.

"It's getting late," he started.

"I wanted to thank you for what you did for Maya," Byron interjected, his amber eyes dark beneath the black slashes of his eyebrows. "If I had known what Pyotr was up to, I wouldn't have allowed Maya to go there."

He wanted to mention that he hadn't exactly allowed Maya to go anywhere. He had ordered her to go to Pyotr, had sent her there like some damned present, a gift he could do as he pleased with.

Maya shot him a worried look, and it was enough to have him holding his tongue again and keeping the peace between him and her brother.

She was with him now, and if everything went to plan, she would stay at his side forever.

"It would be good if you were to stay a night or two, because I have a celebration planned." He weathered the grim look Byron gave him.

"I hardly came all this way for one night."

"Byron," Maya snapped, her dark eyebrows pinching in a frown.

He drew a deep breath and sighed as he looked at her. "I said I wasn't leaving until I'm sure it's safe for you and I meant it."

Safe for her?

August glared at the bastard.

The tether on his temper frayed and his control frayed with it.

"I don't need to prove myself to you… I only have to prove myself to her… she's a grown female. She can make her own decisions." He stood sharply, anger burning hot in his veins, stoked by what Byron clearly thought about him. The black-haired male countered him, rising to his feet and coming to face him, his expression hard. Unapologetic. August growled at him. "I'm not going to hurt Maya. She's safe here, with me. I would never let anything happen to her. I fucking love her."

Byron stared at him.

Maya did too.

August looked down at her, heart pounding, nerves rising swiftly to engulf him. Not quite the way he had wanted to tell her.

"Let's get you settled for your stay." Dalton snatched Byron's arm and tugged him towards the door.

The male tiger stared at August, shock written across his face that matched what he could feel in Maya, until Dalton cleared the steps and disappeared into the night with him.

Maya continued to stare at him, her wide amber eyes as bright as her orange woollen jumper in the light from the fire.

Cold air swept in behind him, stirring her black hair.

"It's beautiful up here at night. I could show you," he blurted, saying the first thing that came to him because he needed to say something.

Anything.

She nodded.

He gathered her coat and helped her into it when she stood, and put his own jacket on as he followed her to the door and down the steps.

She waited for him at the bottom.

He hesitated only a second before taking her hand and leading her towards the broad area at the edge of the plateau to his left, where the fire blazed brightly in the darkness. A gathering place in the village that would be full of noise tomorrow night if everything worked out.

Her steps slowed as they passed the fire and left the halo of light it provided, and she looked up, her eyes taking in the night sky that stretched above them.

Gods, she was beautiful.

"I've never seen so many stars," she whispered and glanced at him.

"It's like this all the time up here." He looked up at the striking band of the Milky Way above them, glittering with a million stars, but it couldn't hold his attention as it normally did.

His eyes dropped back to Maya.

"You might have gone a little over the top with the clothing," he said with a smile as he took in the sight of her swamped in the thick coat and jumper, and her waterproof trousers. It looked as if she had more layers underneath them, and he swore she had been wearing a pair of thinner insulating gloves beneath her waterproof ones earlier.

She smiled back at him, her eyes bright as the firelight caught them. "I was a bit hot by the fire."

"I feel a bit hot now," he husked and looked her over, loving the way she blushed. Maybe he hadn't screwed things up with his blurted confession after all. "What I said—"

"I love you too."

His heart kicked hard in his chest.

He stared at her.

Unsure what to say.

She fidgeted with the zipper on her jacket, glanced at her boots, and then turned to face him and tipped her chin up, all of her nerves gone, replaced by a fiercely determined look.

"You mentioned a celebration… what is it you're celebrating?"

She could have picked a better topic if she had wanted to make small talk to ease both of their nerves.

His shot into overdrive.

"It's still in the works." He struggled not to trip over the words as he fought for the courage to say the things he had been practicing in his head all day. "There's one little detail I need to work out first."

Her black eyebrows rose. "What is it?"

He tamped down another sickening wave of nerves and took a step towards her, closing the distance between them.

She was so damn beautiful, stole his breath just as she had stolen his heart, and all he could think about was her.

Gods, he had spent the past century intent on never being tied to just one female, focused on never settling down and forever playing the field, foolishly thinking that was what he wanted.

Now, he knew what he truly wanted. He wanted one female.

Maya.

"I need to ask you something… and it doesn't have to be now… I don't want you to feel I'm forcing you into anything, because I would never do that… so whenever you're ready, then I'll be ready too, and—"

She stepped into him, hooked her hand around the back of his neck, lured his head down to hers, and breathed against his lips.

"Just ask me already."

He smiled at the way she said that, determined and forceful, a female who knew what she wanted and he had the feeling what she wanted was him.

As her mate.

And she would stop at nothing to make that happen.

"Be my forever?" he whispered, blood thundering in his ears, all hope pinned on her as he waited with bated breath to hear her answer.

She brought her lips up to his.

"Gods, I thought you'd never ask."

She kissed him before he could say something about her tone and tease her back, obliterating his ability to think straight. He swept her up in his arms, his heart singing, soul rejoicing as he held her in them and kissed her, as her words rang around his head, her sweet voice laced with desperation and relief, telling him that she wanted this too.

She wanted to be his mate.

He twisted her into his arms, looping one beneath her bent knees and one around her back, and kissed her as he carried her towards his cabin.

Towards their home.

Before he could reach it, she moved in his arms, breaking free of his hold, and his growl died on his lips when she pressed her chest to his, looped her arms around his neck, and wrapped her legs around his waist, and seized control of the kiss.

As he mounted the steps of their home, his thoughts drifted back to that day in the gym at Underworld, when he had tried to make her submit to him. He might have pinned her then, but in the end, she had been the victor.

She had stolen his heart as her prize.

Claimed it forever as her own.

She dropped from his arms as they entered the house, closed the door behind him and pressed him back against it, her kiss fierce and commanding, bending him to her will.

He surrendered to her.

Always would.

Because she was his whole world, everything he truly wanted and all that he needed.

His beautiful fated one.

"I love you, August," she murmured against his lips between kisses.

He gathered her into his arms and she didn't resist him this time when he lifted her, carrying her towards the stairs.

"I love you too, Maya." He held her gaze, needing her to see he meant every word, and how much she meant to him.

Tonight, he was going to show her how much he loved her, how much he needed her, and that they were meant to be.

Tomorrow, they would celebrate the start of their forever.

A snow leopard alpha and his beautiful impossible mate.

The tiger who had tamed him.

The End

ABOUT THE AUTHOR

Felicity Heaton is a New York Times and USA Today best-selling author who writes passionate paranormal romance books. In her books she creates detailed worlds, twisting plots, mind-blowing action, intense emotion and heart-stopping romances with leading men that vary from dark deadly vampires to sexy shape-shifters and wicked werewolves, to sinful angels and hot demons!

If you're a fan of paranormal romance authors Lara Adrian, J R Ward, Sherrilyn Kenyon, Kresley Cole, Gena Showalter, Larissa Ione and Christine Feehan then you will enjoy her books too.

If you love your angels a little dark and wicked, her best-selling Her Angel romance series is for you. If you like strong, powerful, and dark vampires then try the Vampires Realm romance series or any of her stand alone vampire romance books. If you're looking for vampire romances that are sinful, passionate and erotic then try her London Vampires romance series. Or if you like hot-blooded alpha heroes who will let nothing stand in the way of them claiming their destined woman then try her Eternal Mates series. It's packed with sexy heroes in a world populated by elves, vampires, fae, demons, shifters, and more. If sexy Greek gods with incredible powers battling to save our world and their home in the Underworld are more your thing, then be sure to step into the world of Guardians of Hades.

If you have enjoyed this story, please take a moment to contact the author at **author@felicityheaton.com** or to post a review of the book online

Connect with Felicity:
Website – http://www.felicityheaton.com
Blog – http://www.felicityheaton.com/blog/
Twitter – http://twitter.com/felicityheaton
Facebook – http://www.facebook.com/felicityheaton
Goodreads – http://www.goodreads.com/felicityheaton
Mailing List – http://www.felicityheaton.com/newsletter.php

FIND OUT MORE ABOUT HER BOOKS AT:
http://www.felicityheaton.com

Printed in Great Britain
by Amazon

21204705R10082